LUNA STATION
QUARTERLY

Issue 055 | September 2023

Editor-in-Chief
Jennifer Lyn Parsons

Editors
Katrina Carruth • Sara Doan • Cathrin Hagey
Carly Racklin • Shana Ross
Katrina Schroeder • Gô Shoemake
Bridget Siniakov • Izzy Varju

LUNA STATION PRESS
NEW JERSEY

Luna Station Quarterly publishes short fiction on March 1st, June 1st,
September 1st, and December 1st. For more information and submission
guidelines, please visit our website at lunastationquarterly.com

For Luna Station Press

Creative Director - Tara Quinn Lindsey
Editor-in-Chief & Founder - Jennifer Lyn Parsons

www.lunastationpress.com
LUNA STATION PRESS

CONTENTS

Editorial

Jennifer Lyn Parsons

Jennifer Lyn Parsons is a writer and senior software engineer. Currently, she enjoys writing fantasy stories about middle-aged people who aren't into the whole "going on a quest" thing but do it anyway. When not writing code or prose, she is also the editor-in-chief of the venerable Luna Station Quarterly. She finds joy in baseball, tea, discovering music new and old, and making analog things.

I just came inside after a walk around the yard. This house happens to be on about a quarter acre of property full of long-established landscaping, some of it planted at least a hundred years ago, when the house was built. It's an amazing yard, one of the most biodiverse I've ever seen, particularly in the varieties of plants and fungi we see popping up.

Currently, the back portion has been made even more magical through the use of a lawnmower. One of my family members, our resident naturalist, Elizabeth, has allowed that section of lawn to grow a little wild and then carved out a meditation labyrinth from the numerous types of grasses and weeds.

Yes, I now have access to a labyrinth. It is not made of hedge, but it has quickly become a place where I lose myself, if only for a little while. It doesn't have a monster at the center, instead there is a weather station. It is green and secluded and a place where my mind finds a bit of repose of late.

When you walk a meditation labyrinth it is a different experience than a sitting meditation. Rather than drifting through your inner thoughts before releasing them, you must be more present in the moment from the start. Following the path means your eyes are open, your body engaged with keeping you stable and upright. There is less space for wandering thoughts, though there is a little room for things to surface before releasing them.

I mentioned the uncertainty in my day job. It is temporary, sure to pass more quickly than I think possible while I'm in it. I have also been deep in the process of helping our new editors (Hello to you all!) onboard and start reading the stories that will make up our December issue. I have a lot of plates I'm spinning right now and not a lot of energy left over for myself outside of basic care and maintenance. Really any spare time goes to my family.

This all means that my creative output, which was already almost non-existent, has dropped to nothing. There hasn't even been the space for those background thoughts and story ideas to burble away. That is, until I started walking the labyrinth.

Just a few days ago, I was on the path and thinking about some of my self care options, things I'm trying to do for myself to keep me going. I've been feeling like my mind is full of logic and very little creativity. I was thinking about some old short stories I dug up a few weeks ago and remembered that I wanted to make them into zines. Suddenly, there it was, the creative spark that I thought was dried up for the time being came roaring back.

Zines are a throwback idea, though there is a wonderful crop of new zines out there. I ended up ordering a few to hold me over until I have the space to start creating them again myself. They're such a simple, flexible format; anything that can be printed on paper can be a zine. Stories, essays, art, pictures, comics, whatever. There are zines on positive body image, plant care, poetry collections, and the ultimate meta expression of the form: zines on how to make zines.

The experience of not only holding something tactile in your hands that you created, but also putting the whole thing together is a satisfying exercise in play. Not only can zines be about anything and look however you want, they're also so inexpensive to create that the barrier to entry is incredibly accessible, inviting experimentation as a feature of the format itself. I look forward to playing with them again soon.

I began this editorial talking about labyrinths and landed in zines. That range of disparate topics is not unlike the issue we have for you this time around. There are vampires, aliens, witches, and time travelers, all weaving from one to the other to form the maze of this issue.

I hope you enjoy the journey and when you make it to the center, pay attention to whatever you find there and then follow the path back out. Watch your step and don't get lost. Perhaps leave a trail of breadcrumbs for yourself? We wouldn't want to lose you.

L S Q | 055

Good News, Bad News

Rhonda Parrish

Like a magpie, Rhonda Parrish is constantly distracted by shiny things. She's the editor of many anthologies and author of plenty of books, stories and poems (some of which have even been nominated for awards!). She lives in Edmonton, Alberta, and she can often be found there playing Dungeons and Dragons, bingeing crime dramas, making blankets or cheering on the Oilers.

Her website is at
http://www.rhondaparrish.com
and her Patreon is at
https://www.patreon.com/RhondaParrish.

Ever since the bombs, since the apocalypse, I've become a sort of connoisseur of darkness. They say the Inuit used to have like fifty words for snow and I believe it because given enough time I bet I could come up with fifty words for the dark. It's not just about the degree of darkness, though that's part of it, but also the character of it. The absolute darkness of a new moon has a whole different feeling than the blinding illumination of a full moon off a blanket of fresh snow. And those same levels of light feel completely different if I'm observing them from the safety of home or while out on a scavenge.Tonight the dark feels toothy. It feels hungry.

I remember nights, back in Edmonton when my addiction still held me tight in its fist, which felt like this. Like the shadows were pregnant with potential–all of it bad–and no amount of candles could push back the darkness. There had been fewer such nights since we'd come to Drumheller but tonight was one of them.

I wanted to be back at home, in my little nest in the Dinosaur Hall, but no. Instead of curling up in a mass of blankets and pillows, surrounded by the bones of dinosaurs, I was out here. In the darkness. Surrounded by the bones of humanity.

Broken buildings loomed over me, their jagged shadows elongated and distorted by the light of the nearly full moon. My every step squeaked and crunched in the snow, sounding cartoonishly loud as the sound was amplified and carried by the cold winter air. My scarf was wrapped around my head, carefully so as not to cover my ears or my eyes. I was frightened enough already; to have that fabric distorting my hearing would be unbearable. Ty's ears were covered, and he was comfortable with that, but I thought it was unsafe. If anyone found us out here it could get ugly.

I could hear Ty breathing behind me, see the cloud of condensation that was the physical manifestation of that breath. He was nervous too.

"Do you see it, Papillon?" he asked. His Quebecois accent was smooth, his whisper low.

"I see it," I said. I took a step back from where I'd been peeking around the corner of one building, across the street at another. "Do you want to look?"

He nodded and we swapped places. While he took his turn scoping out our destination I adjusted my scarf to keep the wool that had been dampened by my breath from pressing up against my skin and freezing. After a couple moments he ducked back around the corner.

"Looks abandoned," he said.

"I don't trust it."

"Me either."

***

When we'd arrived in Drumheller I'd been about as miserable as a person could be—an addict detoxing at the end of the world–but when I'd come out the other side I'd seen a reason to go on. To rebuild. Here, in this place where I could see my beloved stars and Ty could be surrounded by the dinosaurs that owned his heart.

After I'd recovered some strength we'd made forays into the city, to scope the place out. Creeping about like mice, darting from the cover of one building to another, we'd made our way through the city. It hadn't been bombed as heavily as Edmonton and more buildings than not were still standing. Everything seemed well picked over though, and most of the people we encountered wore rags for clothing and harried expressions. They scurried about, much like us, with their backs pressed up against the wall. Those few who walked the streets openly were cloaked in bright colours and held long guns against their chests like soldiers from an old war movie.

It took us a good long time before we made it out to the museum. The walls were intact–either it hadn't been targeted by the bombs or they'd missed. The cafeteria and gift shop had been raided, but the exhibits, the bones, they had been left alone. Perhaps the apocalypse had made people appreciate our past, our world's history? Perhaps it was just out of the way enough to not be worth the hassle? Or maybe everyone had been too busy living day-to-day to bother looting the place.

A handful of people had taken to living there in a loose casual kind of companionship. They were comfortable enough that the guards let us in based solely on a patdown and our assurance that we meant them no harm. That was one of the first things Ty and I worked to change once we I decided to set up and make our home there. They were willing to follow our lead, more or less, because they had no other leader among them, and also because of Rex.

All the gasoline hadn't been used or evaporated then, and Rex was the closest thing to a tank any of them had ever seen. Ty had created it back in Edmonton to get us safely out of the city —through the areas of wasteland, the packs of wild dogs and the gangs. It had served us well and now, in our new home, it continued to do so. With Rex we could venture deeper into the city on scavenging trips. Could bring home more.

Most cars and trucks couldn't navigate the streets well because of detritus, other vehicles and man-made obstacles. Motorcycles could, more or less, but they weren't enclosed and you couldn't carry as much on them as with Rex which just rolled over most smaller obstacles and pushed the bigger ones out of the way.

It was ironic, I think. Dinosaurs were wiped out by a thing which fell from the sky and changed their climate so that they couldn't survive. Then we built a civilization out of the oil they became only to be faced with our own climate changing so that we could no longer survive as we had. And then, instead of adapting, we reacted by dropping bombs–from the sky–onto each other until we could no longer survive.

And then Ty and I built our new lives among their bones.

I had a strong back and worked hard. Cleaning things up. Building up security. Scavenging what I could. It sure beat dancing for food, batteries and Bite like I'd done back in Edmonton.

Ty's science background allowed him to put the laboratories and other facilities at the museum to good use creating a hydroponic system, getting the solar power system back online and collecting an obscene number of rechargeable batteries we could charge with solar power and store for a rainy day. Literal or otherwise.

And the other people and the museum came to trust us, and we grew together as a family. As a village, really. We became our own little fiefdom, I guess, like all the others that had carved up the city, but with fewer guns and no colour-coordinated clothing.

And as long as no one caught us scavenging in their part of the city they left us alone, and as we began to deepen our roots and build out infrastructure we needed to trespass into their areas less and less.

Until tonight.

But this was important. The kids needed it. We all needed it.

I peered around the corner at our destination just across the street. The intersection looked empty, as far as I could tell. Pretty even. As I watched a light snow began to fall, big fat flakes that drifted slowly down, looking soft and fluffy in the moonlight. I didn't trust it. It was too easy.

This was Big Zack's territory and he guarded it ferociously. His men were usually armed with baseball bats, and more than a few of them also kept a pistol tucked into their waistband. I'd heard rumours they'd run out of bullets years ago but I didn't want to be the one to test that out, and I didn't want Ty to either. It didn't make sense that he would leave a building unguarded, any building, but especially one that had escaped the bombs completely intact. And stocked. And yet, peering across the street, that's exactly what it looked like.

"Can't be, right?" I asked.

"Unless he's emptied it out, maybe?"

"Maybe." I didn't try to hide my skepticism.

Had there been a visible guard or two I would have gone ahead with our super elaborate plan—namely, sneak around behind them or, if necessary, use the smoke bombs as a distraction and then sneak around behind them—but the absence of guards was setting off alarm bells in my head that I couldn't silence. Going into a risky situation was one thing, walking into a straight-up trap was quite another.

"I kinda wish we'd brought Rex," I said.

We'd left it back at the hospital halfway between here and the museum. In part because fuel was in scarce supply these days, but also because the rumble of an engine attracted a lot of attention these days, which was exactly the opposite of what we were going for here.

"Yes or no, Papillon?" he asked.

This was my idea. My plan. Ty was there to support me, because he was always there to support me, and if I wanted to back out at this point he wouldn't hold it against me. But I wanted to do this. I still believed in it.

Connor and a couple other members of the council thought I was crazy. They didn't think the risk was worth the reward, but I'm confident they'll come to understand once they see. It's not *just* a game.

I adjusted my scarf again, more to give my hands something to do than because it was necessary, and straightened my shoulders. "We've come this far. I say we go in."

"Then we go in." Ty said. I felt his gloved hand on my shoulder and turned to look at him. He peered through the eye hole of his balaclava, his eyes filled with warmth and a confidence I didn't feel. The locations of his mouth and nose were marked by frosty circles in the black wool. "Bad news—this smells like a trap. Good news—at least if this snow keeps up it will cover our tracks."

"Let's do it," I said, and grabbed the towrope for my toboggan. Ty nodded and wrapped the line for his around his wrist a couple times to make it easier to hang onto.

In the absence of Rex we could only take what we could carry on the toboggans. They were extra wide and had sides on them to help contain our booty but we were definitely going to need both of them so that we didn't need to make this trip ever again.

We sprinted across the street. While we were out in the open any number of scouts and snipers (assuming they had bullets) would be able to see us so it was key to make sure we were back in the cover of a building as quickly as possible. Years of scavenging came to our assistance just then as we maneuvered ourselves and our sleds across the street and into the narrow space between two buildings faster than you could say "offside."

Once there, we didn't stop to chit chat but navigated quickly through to the back alley, and the rear door to the sporting goods store. It was locked, of course, but I kept watch while Ty did his thing and less than two minutes later we were ducking inside the store.

It was in remarkably good shape. Still somewhat organized and looking more like a store on stock day than most business which these days looked like they'd had a dozen chimpanzees let loose in them. All the guns and ammo, fishing and hunting gear, were gone, of course, but that was okay. That wasn't what we were there for.

The dark inside was heavy, thick as a Hudson's Bay blanket and just as scratchy. The sound of our sleds dragging against the gritty linoleum floor scraped on my nerves like nails on a chalkboard, and I kept hearing whispers and scuffling that could as easily have been real as imaginary. We found the section we needed soon enough though, and began to load up the toboggans.

Apparently Zack and his men weren't hockey fans. It didn't look like any of the gear had even been touched.

I stacked sticks and pucks onto my toboggan, while Ty grabbed skates, skates and more skates. He snatched them up in every size he could find, stacking the boxes carefully, tying them down with bungee cords and then strapping some more on. We'd decided before coming that we'd have to skip any kind of protective gear. It was just too bulky and we'd need too many sizes to make it feasible, but when I saw rack upon rack of jerseys I couldn't resist. I grabbed two armloads and had just piled them on top of my toboggan when all hell broke loose.

I don't know if it was a flare or a flashgun, but someone used something that turned the dark to a phosphorus white light. It blinded me and made me cry out, stumbling against an empty rack and knocking it over. I clambered back to my feet, eyes slitted against the light and fumbled around on the ground, blindly looking for the towrope attached to my toboggan. I couldn't feel anything through my gloves so I ripped them off and pawed along on the ground.

I could hear the men, coming closer—there were two of them storming through the store toward us.

My fingers wrapped around the rope at the same time as I heard the gunshot. Without thought my eyes opened wide to see two big bodies, dark blotches against a field of white lumbering ever nearer. What they lacked in finesse and speed they made up for in bulk. And bullets.

Another shot rang out and I heard Ty grunt beside me.

"Are you okay?" I shouted.

"Out, out!" he said. He lit the smokebomb–a handful of wooden matches bundled together and bound with electrical tape–by scraping the matchheads against the sandpaper he kept glued to his belt, and threw it with his left hand. It flew awkwardly toward the goons charging toward us, but landed in a pile of boxes that had been stacked on the floor.

I was already dashing back toward the rear exit and the alley we'd entered through, but when I saw the boxes catch fire, little flames licking at their edges, I sped up.

Fire is one of the worst things about the end of the world–there's no one around to put it out. Once, back in Edmonton, there had been a fire that started in a trash can someone had lit to stay warm. That beast had burned for two weeks before there was a snowfall heavy enough to put it out. No one messed with fire.

Once I felt the cold air slap my face–my scarf had come loose and been lost somewhere in the store–I opened my eyes. Both Ty's toboggan and my own were miraculously still loaded. Not perfectly, and no longer neatly, but the bulk of the supplies we'd come here to get were still there. Still secured.

"Bad news," Ty said. "I accidentally started a wee bit of a fire."

"I saw that."

"Good news, they were shouting about an extinguisher and now they'll be too busy to follow us."

Still, they weren't the only people who worked for Zack so we darted down the alley, between the buildings and across the street as quick as bunny rabbits. From there we zig-zagged through back lanes and into Left-eye Leon's territory as quickly as possible. There was no way Zack's men would follow us in there, guns a blazing; it would be the same as declaring war. For similar reasons we couldn't stay there long either. We skirted around the border between his and Zack's territory, then cut across the no-man's land near the Badland's Motel.

By the time we got there Tyrone and I were both dragging our asses. It wasn't surprising that I was exhausted, but Ty ran for fun, the weirdo; this should only have been a warm-up for him. As we leaned our backs against the dilapidated motel, gasping and panting loud enough that anyone with two ears could hear us, I turned to study him. He'd pulled his balaclava off at some point, and his face was pale, his lips thin.

"What's wrong?"

"Bad news," he said, gesturing to the upper part of his right arm. I could see that his coat was torn and the area around the hole glistened in the moonlight. "I got shot. Good news. Only barely."

"Shot? Oh my god, Ty, you got shot!"

Until that very moment I hadn't doubted what we were doing was right. Was worth it. But up until that moment I hadn't recognized, really, the danger we were in. But Ty had gotten shot.

"Only barely," he repeated. And I could hear a smile in his voice. I tore my eyes from the hole in his coat to his face and sure enough, he was grinning like an idiot. "Just a scratch."

I held his hand as we made our way over to the old hospital where we'd parked Rex. Luwam ran that, but Ty had helped set up her hydroponic system last year so she owed us one and had promised to look the other way if we parked there tonight. We decided to push our luck a little further and ask her to sew up Ty's battle wound.

As it turned out he was right. It was just a scratch. I felt better having it stitched up all the same though.

When we left the hospital the snow blanketed everything. Thick, deep. It seemed like there was more and more every year, but I've never bothered to measure it to find out. I've been too busy trying to survive. Ever since the bombs all my needs, all my concerns, had been very immediate. Very short term. Trying to figure out the new rules of society and survival didn't leave a lot of time to think about things like weather patterns and snowfall.

The snow is both beautiful and treacherous. And not just for the cold that accompanies it but also what it can hide. Tucked inside with the heater going full bore I drove over something beneath the snow and Tyrone's shoulder bounced off the passenger side door, hitting right where his brand new stitches are. I winced in sympathy. "Sorry."

"Ah, Papillon," Ty groaned. "This was so much easier when you were in the back and I was driving, eh?"

"Maybe for you, Tyrone," I laughed. "I don't remember that ride so fondly." Detoxing tied up in the back of a veritable tank in the middle of an apocalypse is not something I would recommend to anyone.

"But in the end it was good, eh?" he said, shifting so if I hit another bump it won't slam his shoulder into the door. "Happily ever after."

"We're still working on the ever after bit."

Ever after is the hardest part. One thing about the apocalypse you can't appreciate until you're right there, in the thick of it, is how monotonous it is. How boring. Survival is boring. It is. It's like the ultimate rut. Every morning we wake up and do the same things, the same grind, in order to survive. To eat. To stay warm. To stay civilized. Every day. No days off. Without exception.

Even the kids have to contribute. Have chores.

They have school too, of a sort, but they learn far different things than I did when I was in school. Back before the bombs. They learn the signs that an area is radioactive. How to slow the Wasting. How to maintain the hydroponics, the solar. What plants are edible. How to lay snares. How to raise chickens.

But it's the same for them. Every day. Day in and day out. The same damn thing.

It was important, I thought, to give them something to break up the monotony. Something to look forward to. Something to do.

To give them hope, and joy, and something that is just pure fun.

To give them hockey.

We returned to a hero's welcome—Ty especially once they saw his war wound—and it wasn't even twenty-four hours later before we were watching the first game. Two hastily assembled teams in a mishmash of jerseys, stumbled and fell and basically just tried to stay on upright on their skates in the rink we'd made in the parking lot. There was not a lot of skill, and nobody looked likely to become the next Crosby, Cornell or McDavid but, as day slowly turned to twilight there were a lot of laughs.

No one ever talks about the good parts of an apocalypse. The end of one world, one civilization, is also the beginning of a different one. A new one. It's a fresh slate to start building from, and it was important to me that this be a part of that foundation.

They played under the light of the full moon, and despite the fog that cloaked our breath the darkness felt warm and comforting. Like a down comforter. Like home.

Watching the game I elbowed Ty in the ribs. "Good news," I said. "I think they are getting the hang of it. Bad news? We may need to go back and get some helmets."

Lips Like Sugar

Cynthia Gómez

Cynthia Gómez (she/her) is a writer and researcher. She writes horror and other types of speculative fiction, set primarily in Oakland, where she makes her home. She has a particular love for themes of revenge, retribution, and resistance to oppression. She has stories in Fantasy Magazine, The Acentos Review, Strange Horizons, Tree and Stone Magazine, and several anthologies. Her novelette, "The Shivering World," was published in Volume Two of the Split Scream series. You can find her on Twitter at @cynthiasaysboo. She loves to write dark and frightening things while cuddling with her shadow, aka her adorable little dog.

The first thing Viviana noticed, on her first night as a vampire, was how much she wanted to fuck everyone. When she was alive she'd been drawn to the same few types, again and again, and she had always longed for a palate more adventurous, more brave. Now everyone she passed smelled wonderful, the hunger sharpening inside her with every breath, and she wanted to slide her mouth over the softness of every neck and take them all in. She felt her skin waking up, beading with drops of a cold sweat, a feeling she remembered so well from the beginning of her time with Ravi, her ex. Those day-long hikes on misty trails where desire was so strong it pulled them into hollow trees damp and covered with moss. Everyone she saw now under the streetlights was sending her cold limbs thrumming with the want, like a scarlet nail against a metal guitar string, like a theremin.

Wait, she told herself. *Wait.*

On Friday morning at ten her phone screamed her awake in time to slap concealer under her eyes before her Zoom interview. (How did vampires get jobs in the old days?) Sheets hung all over the windows of the messy space that belonged to Ravi's friend Sara, who'd heard of the breakup and had kindly offered up her bedroom while she was backpacking to the middle of nowhere. The lamps of the borrowed room burned Vivi's eyes, but faintly, like the after-mark of a sunburn. The interviewer kept looking at her phone.

"Looks like you've had a lot of different jobs. May I ask if you see yourself being a janitor long-term?" Vivi just nodded, her smile too shallow to show her new baby fangs. *Probably a lot longer than you can imagine.*

"Why did you seek out the night shift?"

Vivi sucked at her teeth, glad the woman's open-necked shirt wasn't within her reach.

"Well, I . . . finally accepted that I'm just a night person. I'm at my best when everyone else is sleeping."

"Like a vampire?"

Vivi had to turn her laughter into a cough.

"And the employer's not a problem? All those bodily fluids?"

"Oh, no." Vivi could feel the blood thumping inside her, as if calling for reinforcements.

Sunday night at nine would be her first shift. Saturday night she walked around Broadway until she found a bar called Este, full of beautiful people, mostly Black and Brown, and she let herself sway in the crowd, taking in all the glistening skins and the glorious smells. She let her own skin prickle with the want if someone brushed against her, but she touched none of them back, these people who almost surely woke up in the daylight. Instead she fixed her eyes on the janitor, a short and thick woman a few years younger than Vivi, with faded tattoos on her neck and breath of sweet mint when she told Vivi where the bathrooms were. Vivi let the intoxication spread her lips into a hot grin, and as if in response she saw a flush descend from the girl's cheeks down to her throat. Less than ten minutes later she was pressing the girl up against the locked door in the janitor's closet, watching the beautiful mouth contort in screams hidden by the thumping bass of Azealia Banks.

When the girl came off work at two a.m. Vivi was waiting, and they took an Uber all the way back to Antioch, straight to the girl's bed ("Lisa. My name is Lisa. Please . . . " she gasped with Vivi's mouth at the swell of her breasts) and after they had drifted in and out of sleep several times Lisa's hands slid along the rolls at Vivi's waist.

"You're so hot."

"Thank you." Vivi wished she could blush.

"I mean, yeah, that too. But you're so hot."

When Vivi's alarm buzzed her awake, she wanted so badly to stay in that place, the air warm and thick, blackout curtains already protecting against the encroaching dawn. But she kissed Lisa's lush mouth goodbye and walked the two miles to BART. The dark platform was covered with bodies waiting for the 4:15 train. Vivi's thirst, still unquenched, was now thick on her tongue and pounding in her head. Wait. Wait. At least the hunger was softer now, thanks to Lisa, although her hands still throbbed with the wish to slide over every body she saw, pulling aside the uniforms, from construction worker to train dweller, feeling the rush of their blood under her bones. Before leaving Lisa's room she'd pawed through a dresser and stolen a pair of pink gloves. Now she pulled one off, and just as she'd planned it the scent of Lisa, encased in the wool, rose into the air from Vivi's naked hand. She rode the whole way home caressing her own face, breathing in the incredible scent perfuming the air. No one even blinked.

By Sunday night her thirst was screaming in her throat as she waited outside Journey Diagnostics for her supervisor, Jesús, a hiccup of a man in a pale blue shirt. He eyeballed her and handed her a uniform, an access card, a ring of keys, yammered about safe lifting techniques while walking them right past the rooms where the blood was stored. Finally he opened a door and inside were rows upon rows of workstations, samples being tested, the maroon liquid nearly glowing in the overhead lights.

When he finally left her alone she gripped the cart in her clutching hands and rolled it into the emptiest row, eyes on her mop, the floor, while the blood was tested and then tossed into biohazard bins. When one of the techs got up for coffee she pushed the cart toward the bin, hard enough to throw it and its contents onto the floor. "Shit!" she said, louder than she needed to, in case anyone could hear, and she knelt down and slid three vials into her bra. She made herself replace the bin on the wall, even though her fingers were grasping for the vials, ready to tear them open and splatter her hands in scarlet that she would have to lick off.

In the narrow bathroom stall she pulled open the first one, and she could smell the danger right away. *You could have told me this stuff yourself, asshole,* she cursed Andre in her head. After he'd turned her, the only thing he'd done to help was getting her the interview here. She'd stolen a phlebotomy textbook to learn about the chemicals used to test blood, including some that might put her to sleep or send her vomiting a maroon puddle onto the tiles. She threw the shining liquid down the toilet. The next one smelled of warm copper, the color a candy-apple red. Her lips closed around the edge of the vial and gulped it in, and she could feel it warming and coating her throat on the way down. She could take her time with the last one, older and duller but rich and sweet all the same, and her eyes in the mirror looked clearer now as she wiped her mouth and got back to mopping the floors.

When her first paycheck came she posted an ad on Facebook (*Do you need a roommate but still want your space? I work nights and I promise I'll stay out of your hair*) that led her to a couple who rented a tiny little house on Peach Street. They both worked graveyard at an airport motel and drove days for Amazon, and for a rent she could just afford she could have their converted laundry room for fifteen blissful hours a day, Dollar Store sheets tacked up over every window, three layers deep. At her next paycheck she bought real blackout curtains and treated Lisa to an Uber home from Este, Lisa half asleep and half moaning at the tug of Vivi's lips at her throat. The baby fangs pressed against Lisa's veins but Vivi reminded herself of her promise, the one she'd actually managed to keep in the days since her turning: Do no harm. She'd been raised by a Mexican grandmother in a house littered with crosses and so by the time she was sixteen she'd been holding back her desires for years. Until the afternoon her grandmother came home early to find Vivi and her girlfriend Nidia making out on the couch and her response was, "I kind of knew that. Baby, you left the bathroom a mess. Go clean it up. Nidia, are you staying for dinner?"

The nights she didn't go home with Lisa she wandered into dark places where she could sate her hunger, but never her thirst. She was fascinated by the effect her desire had on its objects, the way its power seemed to intoxicate her and them both. There was the barber who blew the last of the hair off her neck and then pulled down the shades and bent her over his green leather chair. The woman in the white sweater and flat shoes who smelled like night-blooming jasmine, who protested, "Aren't I a few decades too old for you?" as Vivi slid aside the damp wool and tasted the woman's neck. Vivi loved the sweet tension of pulling her swelling fangs away from their veins. She loved curbing the strength that she was thrilled to feel pushing through her skin, which in defiance of all myths had remained its same rich brown, except for the black circles under her eyes when her thirst was at its peak. She wondered if it would always feel this exciting, this knowing she could have nearly anyone she wanted, the intoxication that came from walking into places full of strange drunk men and knowing that she was nobody's prey.

One night before work she walked right into a coffee shop and sat across from the kind of man she had never bothered with before, slim and pale and shy, enormous headphones around his ears making him look like a hungry insect. He took her back to his apartment overlooking Beeryland and they ignored his roommates banging on the door for them to quiet down. While she was putting on her uniform she could hear the roommates' dramatic argument, something about Instagram photos and why one of them hadn't proposed yet. She realized how little she missed that life, maybe how little she'd ever wanted it. Memories of when she was alive were drifting away fast, but she remembered how unmoored she had always felt from the world. Her roots had been so shallow and thin even after thirty-one years, leaving nothing for anyone to hold onto, not even Ravi, a man who could make anything bloom.

She kissed the shy man goodbye at the door, his blood smelling delicious, and another roommate (how many of them were there, anyway?) looked over her work uniform and laughed: "Who's slumming?" And a desire rose in her from somewhere that was neither hunger nor thirst. She pictured herself pulling the roommate into a bathroom and pushing down his boxers, tongue and teeth landing on the vein pulsing in the thickest part of his thigh. The life leaving his body, his head rolling back. "Do no harm," she whispered, and left that apartment behind, running her tongue over her baby fangs as the elevator took her down. The fangs liked to poke through even at the most inconvenient times, but they would retract if she concentrated hard. She made herself read the elevator repair certificate and the package theft warnings and anything else within sight, and by the time she was back out on the street she looked normal to the outside world, nothing to see.

Back on Peach Street she started to hear whispers from her house-mates, rumors that the landlord was planning to sell. Vampires in movies never got eviction notices, never had to worry about packing up those velvet-lined coffins that she was pretty sure were a myth. She slept just fine without one. And of course they were always rich, money always flowing into the cracks of their existence. Like the one between their unchanging faces and the dates on every official document they had, a gap that for Vivi was narrow enough now but would widen every year. Lisa was undocumented; that dark space was where she lived.

At work, there were dangers of a different kind. She could manage on only one vial a shift, but she didn't dare steal more than four at a time, the most that would fit into her bra. So many nights she was lucky to end up with one she could actually drink. Then there was the tiny thread of hallway just outside the bathrooms, where sometimes she was careless, starting to drink before she was safely inside. One night she was pulling away the lid of a vial when behind her she heard a cough. It was the shift supervisor, Jesús. She dropped the vial and in the clatter of the plastic onto the floor she could hear all of it: the click of the handcuffs, the cell door locking her in for days or weeks with no relief for her thirst. The sunlight on her skin the first time she had to show up for court, the blisters erupting across her face and her hands. The smile on Jesús' face was thin and wet.

"Did you think you were the only one?"

Relief flooded through her, hot and fast, and the words practically tumbled over each other on their way out of her mouth: "Of course that's what I thought! I haven't met any others yet, just the one who turned me . . . see, I was lonely after I broke up with my ex and I went on a Tinder date and it was this guy Andre, maybe you've met him? Anyway I convinced Andre to turn me instead of–I mean, you know, of course–and then he did and I then asked him what do I do now but he said he wasn't a fucking tour guide so I've been figuring all this shit out on my own and–"

"Whoa, slow down, sister. You don't need to go telling everyone about your Tinder life. I mean, I might not mind, but we'll get to that. Also, why blood? There's much more of a market for piss, but careful, they watch that real close." And the flood of relief was cold water now, soaking through her limbs. He handed her the vial and the smile on his face was like the wolf who's told the girl that she'll be in real trouble for wearing that bright red cape, but don't worry, he won't tell a soul.

Jesús began showing up in the same hallway as Vivi multiple times a week, his eyes always sweeping over her shirt, no matter how loose she began to wear them. The other women on the night shift warned Vivi away from him, and she noticed the way their voices got higher and weaker as they told her, their eyes suddenly sweeping down to the floor. They showed her the pictures he'd sent them, thumbs blocking out what she shouldn't see. They couldn't tell HR; they needed this job. And when two days later the picture came in from him, the text following, "sure you don't want to help me with this?" she knew she couldn't either. Jesús seemed to have a homing beacon for the women who couldn't afford to speak up. And the next time she saw him he brushed up against her in the hallway and she could feel something against her hip, and when the revulsion and fury drained away something else poured into its place, like the feeling from the man who laughed at her uniform, but so much stronger that Vivi's fangs pressed against her parted lips. She closed her eyes and envisioned herself lifting Jesús three feet off the floor, his feet dangling uselessly in the air. *Do no harm*, she reminded herself, *and anyway you can't kill your boss and still expect to get your paycheck.*

The days grew shorter and sometimes she spent them with Lisa, the two of them huddling over Vivi's cracked laptop, watching the baking and house hunting and wedding planning shows that Lisa loved and Vivi couldn't stand. Lisa teared up when the happy couple would step out into the lights, frothing gowns gleaming. She loved to draw, big-eyed women in swirling dresses and sparkly shoes, and Vivi noticed that the women in the drawings slowly began to look more like Lisa herself. She liked to pull Lisa in front of the bathroom mirror, with its horrible fluorescent light, and murmur to Lisa how beautiful her skin was, all of it, and she would watch Lisa's spine straighten and her breath come shallow and fast. She would borrow Lisa's phone to look up "fashion design schools" and "online fashion degrees" to make the ads pop up in her absence, planting a seed.

All the same, the cracks were beginning to show, the arguments already repeating themselves. "Why do you *never* want to meet my friends?" Lisa complained when Vivi refused, again, to go play soccer at Jacobsen Park.

"That's not true. I've done stuff with them."

"One time. You went to drinks with us once."

Tell them to stop planning so much shit in the daytime, Vivi knew she couldn't say.

Then there were all the times she left Lisa's apartment in the dark, never staying for breakfast, saying she was in a hurry, that she wasn't hungry. And then there was the freedom Vivi still went out to taste. She kept telling herself she'd stop when it got boring, when she felt done. She hadn't yet.

Even so, Lisa had begun weaving a daydream out loud, of some cute little apartment an easy train ride away from Este, the two of them spending mornings in a tangle of limbs and then going out in the bright of the afternoon to walk their dog, some fluffy little thing Lisa would spoil with kisses. Vivi could feel the truth longing to push itself through her skin. She tried to imagine it, going down on one knee, the way some people might hold out a little box with a ring or maybe a shiny new house key, except that in hers was a vial of blood. And then she would pull Lisa onto her lap: "I have something I have to tell you." Something Lisa wouldn't believe, the way Vivi hadn't believed it herself, not until the pain howled its way through her limbs, turning her skin thirsty and cold.

One night in early December Vivi showed up at Este at closing time as she often did, to find Lisa waiting for her with a bag of Vivi's stuff. "I know you never lied to me. You said you could never promise to only be with me. And I said I was okay with that, but–" she sucked in a breath, making her face passive, this girl who cried at reality shows– "I don't think I am. Not anymore. Do you think we could . . . "

Vivi closed her eyes, feeling the tears roll over her cold cheeks. Here was Lisa summoning all her courage to ask for what she needed, even if the answer was "no." Vivi knew that the end had to come sometime, that someday the cracks would be too wide for either of them to reach across. And here it was, come way too soon. Too soon for that little vial, to ask Lisa to give up every sunrise for the rest of her days. And hadn't Vivi done so much of this when she was alive? So many promises she'd made to Ravi, to the lovers before him, promises she'd always thought she could keep.

The two of them held each other until Lisa's Uber pulled up, and Vivi walked the seven miles home with the weight of the canvas bag over her shoulder, the bag that Lisa had packed and had ready because she'd kind of known what the answer would be.

Then a week later Lisa showed up at Peach Street without texting, just like in the old movies, and Vivi threw a hoodie over her head and hid her arms inside her sleeves and bit off the gasp as a strip of sun hit her exposed hand. They were diving under the covers before the laundry room door even shut, and she could pretend they were in a safe cocoon, these borrowed sheets in a borrowed bed in a rented house with For Sale signs popping up all up and down the block. She poured mimosas for them both, tossing her own down the sink when Lisa's back was turned, and then Vivi lay there watching her dream, feeling the pulse of Lisa's blood in her neck, marks in the shape of a mouth on Lisa's throat, like sugar spots on a peach, the room filling with the scent of her, and Vivi had never thrummed more with desire in her life. Or after it.

Two nights later Vivi stood on the Coliseum platform, not shivering in the chill. She needed to sneak in to work a little early, see if she could steal a quick drink. Lisa was sending flurries of texts, none of them touching the distance that still yawned between them, the questions neither of them wanted to ask. Was there a future where that little box might live? Or were they just spooling the end even longer behind them both, making sure it would only bleed harder when the thread finally had to be cut? The images Lisa was sending made Vivi glance over her shoulder, glad she couldn't blush. She started typing: *how many can I give you this time?*

And then the picture crawled across her screen. This wasn't Lisa; this was Jesús, and she could feel the nameless desire stabbing into her ribs, stronger than hunger, stronger than thirst. She let herself imagine the release of finally, finally letting her new fangs serve their use, how sweet her thirst would feel when it was just about to be quenched. She imagined his blood still warm as it coursed into her mouth, and she slid her thumb over the screen of the phone, back and forth. She had plenty of time before she had to clock in. Another text came in: *You sure? No roommates...I live alone.*

Back in September, when she'd swiped right on Andre's profile ("I like hot nights and cold days") it wasn't only for sex, but also for a night away from a bedroom borrowed from a friend of her ex, the awkwardness of feeling both unwelcome and grateful. It was delicious to see Andre's face when he realized she wasn't afraid of his fangs, but instead saw something she wanted. It wasn't so much the thought of eternity. It was never again wondering how she'd pay for both rent and food in the same month, no more worrying about checkups and fillings and the specter of hospital visits she could never pay for anyway, the cost of maintaining a body that would still get weaker and sicker and old. The ability to finally walk at three a.m. in joyful solitude and without fear. "But I won't become a killer," she'd sworn, half-contorted in pain, begging for Andre to finish the turning.

His laugh was cruel. "That's what I said too. But once you open that door, it's going to want to stay open."

"I mean it," she'd told him, her voice weak and thin. He'd regarded her carefully. "Maybe you do." And then he'd leaned in to finish the job, her blood fresh on his mouth.

The speakers crackled overhead; the train would arrive at 7:09. Jesús was taking her silence for consent and kept sending pictures. *You might want to rethink that,* she wanted to tell him. And then the next picture came in, and she could tell from the shapes in the window behind him just what building he was texting her from. She'd been in that very building, in fact, on one of her roving nights out, a crumbling thing with dark hallways and a front door that didn't close. She could find his apartment number from a mailbox, a package left in the lobby. He wouldn't know she was coming until she was already there. She could drop her phone on the train floor, no trace to lead back to her. Maybe she'd only warn him, drawing just enough to leave him feeling dizzy and weak. And afraid. "This is what happens when you can't keep it in your pants," she could shout behind her as she slammed his front door.

"Who's gonna believe you?" he liked to say to women when he rubbed up against them in the halls. "Careful with that, Jesús," she told the empty air. "They might not believe you, either." She licked her lips. The train was coming.

The Very Hand of God

Ellen Morris Prewitt

Ellen Morris Prewitt once decorated her house in honor of Godzilla. She works supernatural elements into her work without realizing it. Her fantasy THE BONE TRENCH about Mother Mary hot-footing it to earth with her snarky Guardian Angel to find her missing son—which one reader said managed to offend everyone but terrorists—was a Short List Finalist in the William Wisdom-William Faulkner Novel-in-Progress contest.

On that first day, when the Memphis sun was burning Craig Avenue like toast left too long in the toaster, Eugene caught a glimpse of it. A delicate bubble of spit, pinkened by aching gums or the thin trace of blood inside a slapped cheek. The sun caught the dab's beveled edge and showed it to be hard. Hard but polished.

Eugene leaned then squatted.

His baggy pants ruffled at his calves.

He plucked the glass from the curb. The droplet was no bigger than the crystals of sugar that coated the rock candy Eugene sucked when he was little, ambling down the sidewalk, happy as a June bug. That was when the neighborhood and Eugene had been young, before he'd grown up and married Lavinia and raised little Rande in the house on Craig. In those days, he and Lavinia stood at the bay window and watched Rande and the other neighborhood children swinging on rope swings, playing race car in cardboard boxes, whatever kids did for fun.

Gradually, the happiness seeped away as first one then another family moved out. When the school where Eugene once taught closed, the neighborhood died a slow, strangled death. Businesses shut their doors, sidewalks developed cracks that went unfixed.

The last business holding on—the gas station on the corner with its dinging bell—finally fell silent. What was once loved became ignored, and the tips of Eugene's black hair turned to white like frost resting on fallen leaves. So long ago.

On his palm, the pink glass twinkled.

Eugene laid the hardness on his tongue.

Not sugar.

Back on his palm, wet now. "Glass," he said but that didn't seem like enough. "Glassiness," he added, in honor of his teaching days. Back then, while his wife worked the night shift at the hospital, Eugene would grade his students' papers under the glow of the standing lamp in the living room until it was time to click off the light and tuck into bed. He and Lavinia cheered when their son turned to the ministry, celebrated when Rande and Judy married, mourned when the new parents announced that family gatherings would take place at their house from now on 'cause all that plywood on the windows in the old neighborhood, it just wasn't good for the grandkids.

Eugene held the glass over his bag and released it. As it fell, the glass twisted in the air and caught the light, its color the same as the skin on a baby rabbit. Satisfied, he straightened and saw a second shard glittering amongst the weeds that sprang from the cracked asphalt. As he bent to collect the second slip of pink, he saw a third dot embedded in the gravelly dirt.

That's when Eugene knew he was on to something.

***

The glass wasn't there every day. Oh, yes, Eugene began to

search but acting nonchalant, as if it didn't matter, sneaking up on it, palming and bagging, adding it to his collection.

Because it was becoming a collection.

Every object Eugene found in his wanderings up and down Craig he laid on the counter in the garage. Musing, he would arrange the objects into a puzzle, a shape, maybe, of a dancing man with a broken belly, arms akimbo, too-round head. Then he'd wrap it in tin foil and lay the packet high on the garage shelf. When the packs counted ten, he tied them together with string. He knew that when he passed, his preacher son would finally show up at the house and unwrap every single pack, smudging dirt on his fancy preacher's suit, convinced that somewhere in one of those darn packets was a thing worth saving.

Eugene did not store the pink glass in the garage. He protected it in a Mason jar on his bedroom dresser. Soon, the bottom of the jar was covered with clinking glass.

"Gene, honey, what are these?"

Lavinia lifted the jar, rattled the glass.

Eugene, getting ready for bed in the bathroom, stopped brushing his teeth, let the toothpaste drip from his mouth into the sink.

"Glass," he muffed out, his mouth full of foam.

And that was all he offered, for he'd stopped sharing his more delicate thoughts with his wife ever since the afternoon several months ago when he'd discovered her—hand on hips—in the garage. "What's in those?" she had asked, pointing to the packets of tin foil.

"My findings," he said, and told her about the hot asphalt, the lonely stretches, the cool shade of the overpass.

Lavinia had stared at him a moment, then fingered open one of the packets. She displayed her palm to him, her hand full of his rusted objects. "Are you turning into an old-man bag lady, Eugene? Collecting worthless junk nobody wants?"

He let her grumble on about shelf space and kept his mouth shut. After all, he'd gone to the streets to keep from being underfoot. Seemed instead of solving the problem of their relationship, he had wedged the two of them further apart.

Tonight, while he spit and rinsed, she humphed. When he crawled in between the cool sheets of their bed, she was still standing, arms crossed, frowning at the glass.

"Magic beans," she muttered. "You're living in a Jack-and-the-Beanstalk world, Eugene." She cricked her neck in his direction. "You're thinking you found some kind of answer with this glass business. There's never been no such thing as magic beans."

Eugene turned his face to the wall.

He did not need his preoccupied wife pronouncing on his life.

***

Over the next few weeks, the sprinklings of glass grew. Where once the pink had appeared only around the curb, its sparkle now shone at the four-way stop sign, over by the sewage grate, and finally all the way to the line of scraggly magnolias dying in the sun. Eugene always avoided the spindly trees with their shriveled leaves, but the twinkle called him over.

He'd follow the twinkle anywhere.

As Eugene walked and searched, it seemed to him the glass was sprinkled by the very hand of God. Hesitantly at first, then in wider—and more reckless—arcs.

Gone was the Mason jar on the dresser top. In its place stood a gallon pickle jar, replaced by a two-gallon mayonnaise jar, replaced again by a five-gallon salad dressing jar from the Dollar Store, even though Lavinia made it good and clear she would throw up if she ever again had to take another bite of Thousand Island dressing.

"For the glass," Eugene said.

Lavinia rolled her eyes.

But, to himself, Eugene worried. What jar—clear glass so that you could see the pale shards piled inside—was larger than a five-gallon dressing jar? Eugene roamed the aisles at the Dollar Store, mingling with the skinny boys who should've been in school, their faces sprouting acne, skin pale as a fish's belly. But it wasn't until he was standing on Craig Avenue next to the four-way stop that he found a bigger jar.

Sitting straight up.

Bristling clean.

The jar was waiting for him.

Its bottom was good and fat, its neck stretched thin. The jar must have been three feet high. Put there, Eugene thought, to be picked up by him.

And he did—he picked it up and toted it home.

When he arrived, carrying the wonderful jar, tilting its handsome neck so the jar would fit through the front door, who was there with Lavinia but Rande.

"Dad, we need to talk," Rande said, and sat his ample behind down on the living room sofa.

The boy sat so earnest, leaning forward in his black suit, his forearms on his thighs. All grown up, hair slicked down, an important preacher at a big ol' church in the suburbs, leading his sheep in the way of the Lord. His son knew how to approach a troubled soul.

At least that's what his face was saying to Eugene.

"Talk about what?" Eugene asked. "'Cause if it has to do with the glass, I'm doing fine on my own." The tone of his voice reminding his son how seldom he came down to visit and never brought Judy and the young uns. How when he did appear, he was always swiping at his suit, acting like the old neighborhood was soiling his clothes.

"Is that what the jar's for?" Rande asked, nodding at the perfect jar Eugene had set on the floor. "For the glass?"

"Naw, it's for you to collect money in next Sunday," Eugene said.

Things went downhill from there.

"Because you were rude," Lavinia said that night after Rande had scurried back to his wife and kids.

"Because that boy is too big for his britches." Eugene rolled over, seeking sleep.

Still, the pink glass kept flipping out of the air like nickels pulled from behind God's ear. Eugene never asked himself who was smashing a big pink thing into thousands of pieces and dribbling it onto the avenue. He didn't ask because he thought he knew the answer, and Eugene wasn't a man comfortable being in cahoots with the Almighty.

So he dribbled his tinkling shards into the wonderful jar, and when it was half-full, he settled it in front of the fireplace.

"That doesn't look so good there," Lavinia said, nodding at the jar that dwarfed the small fireplace. "Cain't hardly see my wreath. Not just big," she added. "Strange."

Eugene shook his head. His wife, just now lifting her eyes from her quilting or her wreath-making or whatever it was that day and realizing his collection of pink ever-growing glassiness glass was strange.

***

The next jar—comical in its size, as if it had once been part of a promotion—was so big it had to go on the front porch. Not many people drove down Craig Avenue anymore, but the folks who chose the old street slowed down to look at the promotion jar on the porch. When the large wine bottle appeared on the lawn, standing almost nine feet tall on the well-mowed grass, they slammed to a full stop.

One of the cars that stopped early on a Monday morning was a reporter from Channel 13 News. She rang the doorbell and waited on Eugene's porch, pretty the way newswomen were these days, young with shiny red lipstick. When Eugene opened the door, the woman pointed to the wine bottle and asked: could she have the story?

"Not one to tell," Eugene replied.

Lavinia, standing in the doorway behind him, said, "Good day to you," reached around Eugene, and tugged the door shut.

But the next day, as Eugene walked the street, he caught sight of the reporter hunched behind the wheel of a Honda, trailing behind him. Rounding the block, idling at the corner, finally getting out of the car to walk Craig Avenue on foot. No one but Eugene walked Craig Avenue on foot, except for the hooligans skipping school. So the reporter had nowhere to hide. Still, he avoided her. He didn't want to subject the glass to scrutiny, a private thing between him and whoever was laying it down.

He put her off, moseying two or three blocks from the real finds, the reporter stubbing along behind him. Once, he even braved the nighttime to level the beam of a flashlight across the asphalt, watching for the special wink of the glass.

Then one evening, when he and Lavinia were slumped in front of the evening news, a picture of their front yard sprang onto the screen.

The nine-foot container of pink glass popped in the sunlight.

The girl reporter pointed to the bottle while she talked. She used phrases like "clouded in mystery," "striking as lightning," "glass raining from heaven," making Eugene think maybe she was working her way up from weather girl.

Then she was shown walking the fake search path, talking about where Eugene collected his glass. "An old man," she called him, rude like reporters could be. Lavinia was his "long-time wife."

"What does she know, 'long-time?'" Lavinia huffed.

"Guessed," said Eugene.

After that, the cars coming down Eugene's stretch of Craig multiplied. Big white Cadillacs, black SUVs, mud-splattered pick-up trucks—every make and manner of car idled down the street. Every make, that is, except for Rande's silent sedan.

His son did call. Lavinia answered the phone while Eugene sat in his recliner, listening. Naw, he didn't need to come over, not what with writing his sermon and Judy's choir rehearsals and taking the kids to music lessons. Yeah, serving the Lord sure did keep one busy, and no, it wasn't that big of a deal to be on the news.

After Lavinia hung up, she stood beside the receiver, fiddling with the cord.

"You wanna fix me a ham sandwich?" Eugene asked.

She snapped out of it and, in a minute, here was the ham sandwich and a glass of milk. She brought them out to the porch where Eugene had gone to sit. Handing him the snack, Lavinia slipped into the chair next to him and watched as the cars streamed by.

"Haven't seen this many cars in I don't know when," she said.

"Busy night," he said.

"It's never a busy night round here."

"Busy night tonight."

They sat.

"Enough mustard for you?" she asked. "Or you want a pickle maybe?"

When he didn't answer, she rose slowly and then he was alone.

Eugene, munching on his sandwich and eyeing the traffic, figured the flow would taper off soon as the gawkers understood there wasn't anything left worth gawking at on Craig Avenue.

Not on the street.

Not in his yard.

Not in his life.

They would quit coming when they saw that nothingness.

They always did.

***

Early the next morning Eugene was standing on his lawn in his bathrobe reading the morning paper. On the front page was a story about the police arresting parents whose kids had missed too much school. Shame. Eugene flipped the paper over. Below the fold was an article on the planned revitalization of Craig Avenue.

"We'll make it happen," said the deputy director of the Memphis something-or-another agency. Talked about putting in sidewalks. Over-hauling the utilities. Even mentioned a grocery store. Cited "renewed interest" in the old street as of late.

"I'll be damned," said Eugene as the still-wet grass tickled his ankles.

"Don't think you can stop me."

Eugene glanced up from his reading.

There on his lawn, not two feet from the big jar of glass, was a skinny little boy in a raggedy t-shirt. The boy's arm was heaved back. A heavy rock rested in his fist. The boy wasn't ten years old, big rabbit ears, and still with the buck-teeth of a child, hefting that big old rock, his face contorted with rage.

In another time, the boy would've been one of Eugene's students, seated at his desk, head bent over his math equations. When Eugene asked the class a question, the boy would politely raise his hand. Eugene would smile at his correct answer. Not now.

"You can't stop me," the kid repeated, even though Eugene hadn't made a move.

The boy let loose with the rock, shattering the jar into a thousand pieces and tumbling the glass onto the lawn with a whoosh! The soft pink mound glittered on Eugene's front yard.

A beautiful pot of light.

With an angry kid hovering above.

The boy's mouth stretched thin, his fingers twitched like the destruction wasn't good enough.

He wanted another rock.

Eugene studied the boy's clutching fingers, his peeved face. Mad at a world that had lost sight of him, that wasn't tracking his wants and desires, a world that had done nothing but ignore him. In the boy's contorted face, Eugene saw his own anger. But the boy, at least, had tried to do something about it. He'd tried to make someone notice.

Eugene glanced up and down the street.

"How you feel about rust?" Eugene asked. He hooked a thumb toward the garage. "I got packets and packets into the garage. You wanna take a look?"

The boy squinted.

"For free," Eugene added.

And since most everyone in this world will take whatever you're offering for free even if it's pure junk, the boy looked left, right, then trotted along after Eugene.

Inside the garage, Eugene peeled back the edges of the tin foil packet. The boy laid his finger on the rusted washer.

"My dad was a mechanic," he said. "'Fore the gas station closed."

"Your daddy doesn't want you tearing up other people's property."

The boy slid his little finger into the washer's hole. He raised his hand, admiring the rusted ring. "I hate pink."

"That's no cause."

The boy slid off the washer. He palmed a heavy bolt, and squeezed. When he opened his fist, ridges rose from his skin. "Blood was on my daddy's gums. It ran down his teeth. They turned pink."

Eugene studied the hair needing a cut. Something a daddy was supposed to do for a child. "Is your daddy dead?"

When the boy nodded, a tear pinged onto the tin foil and collected in the crinkles. He laid the bolt in the packet and folded the package into an awkward triangle.

Eugene's palm hovered over the boy's head. Slowly, he rested his touch on the child's shoulder. "Here. Let's you and me go inside and get some milk and a sandwich. You like a ham sandwich? I got a wife makes a good ham sandwich."

The boy shot Eugene a look. "Nobody eats ham sandwich for breakfast."

"Sometimes you gotta do something doesn't make a lot of sense if you want it to work out right."

"Stupid sandwich ain't gonna make it work out right." The boy's cheeks scrunched against the coming tears.

"I'm not saying it is. All I'm asking is, do you want a ham sandwich?"

The boy's blue eyes shut once, twice. He nodded.

Which was how Eugene came to unload his packets of rust, how his wife came to get a clean garage, how his son was saved the humiliation of opening packet after packet of worthless junk. And how everyone was relieved of jarfuls of pink glass.

For, after that, the pink glass stopped falling.

Or maybe Eugene simply quit hunting it. He was far too busy. He and the boy—Andrew was his name—were mortaring a wishing well in Eugene's front yard. A wishing well molded in place and decorated with sparkling pink glass and lovely rusted treasures.

"Trowel," he would say, naming the tool.

"Trowel," the boy repeated.

Then Eugene made sure Andrew cleaned the tools so they wouldn't rust. Anything to make the boy feel useful before he went home to whatever awaited him.

Then Eugene would go inside. There, he and his wife of thirty-seven years—"not long-time"—would call their own son. The father no longer waiting for the son to call. He and Lavinia talked into the phone at the same time, saying hi to Judy and the little ones, catching up on what the family had done that day.

Afterwards they drug their folding chairs into the yard, arranging them beside the pink wishing well. As the sun set and the moon rose in the sky, they'd sit, and sometimes even hold hands.

"Nice about the grocery store," Lavinia said.

"Gas station'll be next," nodded Eugene.

"You'd think so, with all these cars."

"All these cars."

"A gas station with a repair shop."

"Gotta have a repair shop."

A car creeped by. Lavinia rose her hand, encouraging the traveling strangers to toss pennies into the beckoning well. Most folks slowed and tossed, because everyone knew that whatever was collected in the well went to a fund for the children of the neighborhood. Which was a good start. Only Eugene knew that the inexplicable pink-and-rust wishing well could solve problems money couldn't touch.

"Go on, toss it in." Eugene flipped his fingers to show how it was done.

"If you know what's good for you," Lavinia added.

Built for Her

Camden Rose

Camden Rose is a queer author who loves seeking out magic hidden beneath the everyday world. After graduating from Elon University, she brought her typewriter and ideas across the country to Seattle where she now lives with her partner, black cat, and collection of books and board games. You can find her online at camdenscorner.com.

It took weeks to make her, to carve every strand of hair, every scar, every nail and bump and ridge out of the clay. It took even longer to make the heart, to enchant every few centimeters of wire and to bend it in just the right way. But when she was done, Cassandra almost cried. Naomi looked as beautiful as the day she left.

The colored slips were placed perfectly around the body, adding just the right amount of tint. From the long black hair to the emerald-green eyes, the sculpture was an exact replica. If Cassandra was to see the body she made walking down the street, she would think it was really Naomi. All that was left was to bring life into it, to fill the heart with the love of the real Naomi. Love that wouldn't want to leave just because Cassandra had done something stupid.

Cassandra was a skilled sculptor, but to say she was any sort of witch or magician was a stretch. That had been Naomi's thing. Still, when Cassandra found the spell book in the back of a kitchen cabinet, she felt like she had to try. There was no harm in that. And, there was no other option. She had done everything else: calling Naomi, texting her, reaching out in every way possible to apologize and say it won't happen again.

Well, it's already happened once, Naomi's mom answered matter-of-factly when Cassandra showed up at her house in a last-ditch effort. When Cassandra didn't have any response to that, Naomi's mom sighed and closed the door, saying it was time for the two of them to move on so they could be better people.

Instead of taking that advice, Cassandra started building the clay sculpture that night. Carving into it every promise, hope, and desire that she wanted to give the real Naomi. Everything she wanted to do right. And, weeks later, she stood in front of the beautiful sculpture she built to make everything better. It would be better this time.

As Cassandra opened the spell book, the smell of musty pages overtook the scent of clay, the two swirling together in something earthy and old. She pulled at the weathered pages until she got to the one she wanted. She paused, took a deep breath, then clearly and simply repeated the words on the page. The worst case, Naomi didn't come. Cassandra would be exactly where she started. Heartbroken and empty.

The strange and twisting words came to an end as Cassandra's mouth closed with a snap. But Naomi still stood mannequin-like in the center of the studio. Maybe Cassandra had done something wrong. The spell should have returned the love she'd lost—the version of Naomi that existed before that terrible night. Yet nothing happened.

Cassandra closed the book and hugged it against her chest. It was pointless anyways. Naomi, real or clay, would never want Cassandra after what she did.

But then Naomi's arm twisted back like a slot machine, forming unnatural angles that made Cassandra want to look away. The head leaned left, right, left, right, then centered itself in the middle. The painted flesh became more defined, more detailed, as if blood and breath were entering the body. Naomi blinked.

Cassandra's heart stopped. It was hard to remember that this was just clay. That this Naomi didn't know about the night Cassandra had raised her arm without thinking. This Naomi loved her. This Naomi didn't leave.

"Who are you?" Naomi said.

Cassandra put the book down on her crafting bench. Naturally, Naomi was confused. Cassandra just needed to remind Naomi who she was to help her get her bearings.

"I'm Cassandra Hues, your—"

"You look old," Naomi said. She put her hand on her hip, showing sass that Cassandra had never seen before. Maybe it just took time for the personality to settle in.

"I guess? It's been a few months since you...last saw me." She wondered how far the spell had gone back. From what time did it copy Naomi? When was the last time that Naomi had truly loved her?

Naomi looked left and right. Cassandra wished she had closed the studio door, but the heat had just become too oppressive. She wasn't very good at thinking things through. She turned back to Naomi to ask some questions about what day she thought it was, but suddenly Naomi was wrapping her hand around Cassandra's head, kissing her with earthy-tasting lips.

It was intoxicating, having Naomi in her arms again, feeling her body against hers. So intoxicating that Cassandra hardly noticed how the skin felt clammy and cold to the touch, how she could feel the clay that was still too moist sticking to her curls, and how

Naomi was moving her other hand up Cassandra's shirt. When the hand started to press against her breast, Cassandra moved back, breathing heavy. Even in their honeymoon phase, Naomi had acted so much like a hungry teenager. She was deliberate, slow, and intentional. It was one of the things Cassandra missed. She had never dated someone like that. She was the exact opposite of Cassandra in many ways, and that's why they needed each other.

Naomi tilted her head at Cassandra, but backed off. "What was that for?' she said. "We probably only have a few more minutes until your dad is back."

"My dad?" Cassandra scratched her head, getting clay between her hair. Her dad had been dead for years, long before she'd ever met Naomi. And even if that wasn't the case, she hadn't lived with him since she was in high school. "Who are you?"

Naomi shrugged as though it was obvious. "Tiffany, of course. Who do you think I am?"

Instead of responding, Cassandra motioned for Tiffany to look into the mirror to her left. When she did, Cassandra watched Tiffany stroke Naomi's cheek with Naomi's hand, pull at Naomi's hair with Naomi's fingers.

"I think there was some mistake. You're not meant for this body, Tiffany," Cassandra said. She wasn't sure how else to say that she had thought Naomi would be the only one who would enter. The only one who loved Cassandra right.

Naomi's gaze dropped to the floor. Cassandra hated to see Naomi look this sad, and had to keep reminding herself it wasn't her. It wasn't Naomi. It was someone else, someone she hadn't seen for a long time.

Cassandra padded up behind and wrapped her in a hug, before apologizing. Then, she stepped back and plunged her hand through the back of the chest with a wince. Tiffany gasped in shock, her face reflecting in the mirror as though she had been stabbed. Cassandra looked away until she felt the body still. Then, she pulled out the wired heart, trying not to think about how, for a brief moment, Naomi's back was as smooth as skin.

While Naomi's body froze, staring just beyond the mirror, Cassandra pulled at the wired cage, still slick with bits of clay. Strands of metal twisted apart and a golden wisp flew free, vanishing into the air. Cassandra closed the cage again and sniffled. She looked over at Naomi's body, vacant and frozen, a hole right through the center, showing where the cage needed to go.

With a deep breath, Cassandra closed the heart back up, and put it in the chest. Her hands dripped with damp clay, dark streaks running down her arms.

Cassandra only needed a chance to prove that she could get it right. To show that she could be a better person. She turned Naomi around and used her thumb to smooth over the skin, making sure to be careful with her body. She stepped back and the clay figure jolted to life. The arm rotated, the head tilted, the eyes blinked. She stared into the clay eyes and wondered who lay behind them this time. Who else loved Cassandra before Naomi did?

She'd find Naomi even if it took a thousand tries. No matter how many souls the spell brought, there was only one that gave her gentle kisses and laughed as though the world was built for her. There was only one Naomi.

"Casey?" Naomi said.

Only one person had ever called her Casey. Cassandra rubbed her hands on her smock, as if wiping the clay away would remove what she'd done. What she would have to do again.

"Jake," she whispered.

They'd dated in her early 20s. He was ready to settle down, create a life with her. She was not.

"Have you gotten taller, or have I gotten shorter?" he joked with a sly grin. Cassandra had never seen Naomi's face tilt that way. It felt unnatural. Jake was so relaxed about everything, Naomi was not.

Cassandra moved toward him. It was the only way.

"I'm sorry, Jake," she said, but before he responded, she had thrust her hand into his chest, clay bleeding down her arm. It was cold and slippery—the heart—but she managed. He gasped in the same way Tiffany had, the same shock of losing your life to someone you love.

Cassandra pushed the feelings down. She just needed to get to Naomi. Naomi would make her feel whole again. Naomi would make her smile and want to try again. Naomi would force Cassandra to be a better person.

She pulled at the wired cage, metal cutting at her flesh. Eventually, her fingers hooked, and she made a hole big enough for the light red soul to slip through. It disappeared into the air. Cassandra let out her breath. She looked back at Naomi. If she was right, if she could cast spells, this next one would be her. She'd only seriously dated three people.

Carefully, she placed the heart back into the chest and smoothed it over. Then, she stepped back and watched the arm move, the head tilt, and the eyes blink.

"Naomi," she breathed.

Naomi stared at her and Cassandra shifted on her feet. She wanted to take her girlfriend in her arms and apologize for everything, to go back to how things were, but this Naomi wouldn't know anything was wrong in the first place. This was the Naomi that loved her, not the one that left.

"Cassandra," Naomi stated with no inflection. Cassandra shivered. The sculpture spoke with the voice of a corpse. But who else could it have been? She had already faced down her past failures. The lovers she'd abandoned.

"Naomi?" Cassandra asked.

Naomi's mouth twisted into a jeer and she stood straight, her shoulders wide and neck high. Even though Cassandra was still technically taller, she had never felt so small.

"Have you already forgotten about me?" Naomi said. She moved forward, swift and deliberate. Every move looked intentional and strong. Cassandra backed up until she hit the table. The spell had gone wrong. This wasn't her Naomi. Her head reeled.

"I thought, after all the time we spent together," Naomi continued, walking closer and closer, "I thought you'd never forget me."

Naomi was now close enough that Cassandra could smell the clay in her breath. Normally a smell that comforted her, it was nothing but terrifying now. She shrank down on the table and Naomi loomed over her. Only one person had ever treated her like this.

"Abe," she whispered. Had he ever even loved her? They'd been on and off for a few months, but all she remembered was his cruelty at the end. She'd left as soon as she had the chance.

Yet, here he was in the body she'd built for Naomi. Three hundred pounds of clay and wire and magic. She shuddered to think of what he could do now. Just one blow could knock her out, or worse.

She reached for his heart, but Abe smacked her out of the way with Naomi's hand. Cassandra pulled back, clutching her arm to her chest.

"Of course, bitch."

Cassandra couldn't hear anything but her heartbeat, couldn't smell anything but his earthy breath. It surrounded her like a poison. Her mouth felt dry and she swore she tasted blood. She needed to get him out of Naomi's body.

She took her left hand and felt on the table for something to help. When she found the sculpting knife, she grasped it in her shaky fist and brought it forward with a scream. But, when she got close to Naomi's face, she found she couldn't do it. Not to her Naomi. Taking the heart cage out was one thing, but intentionally hurting Naomi was too far. She had promised herself she would never hurt Naomi like that again. She hesitated, the knife above Naomi's head like a sacrifice.

Abe knocked the tool from her hands. It skittered along the concrete floor.

"So, now that that's over, how about we have some fun," Naomi's voice said, honey dripping from each word. Cassandra's chest heaved. She had to get out. She glanced toward the door, still open, then kicked Abe in the leg. It felt like she was kicking a rock, but the clay collapsed beneath her boot.

She darted towards the door as he collapsed. There was a thud as his head hit the sculpting table. She knew she shouldn't have turned, but she needed to see Naomi one last time.

Naomi's face had collapsed like a smashed loaf of bread. Her hair, so carefully placed strand by strand, now jutted out of the dent like a hair job gone wrong. A twisted smile contorted her misshapen face as she lurched past Cassandra and slammed the door shut.

"That wasn't very nice," Naomi said, a slight gurgle to her voice. Cassandra's heart raced. This must be how Naomi felt that night.

"This isn't you. This isn't...it isn't you," Cassandra whispered to herself.

"Of course it's me, Cassandra." Naomi opened her arms with a smirk.

But instead of responding, Cassandra dashed across the garage and grabbed the cutoff wires. She lunged for Naomi, wrapping the wire around the sculpture's neck and pulling. The tool cut through the skin with little effort, causing Naomi's head to start sliding off. Naomi reached up to stop it, and Cassandra forced her hand into Naomi's chest. Naomi's face froze in shock.

The heart was sticky and warm when she pulled it out, a sickly green wisp floating inside. Cassandra looked over at Naomi's body, at the mess it was now, then back at the wisp. It banged against the cage.

She pulled the wires apart and the green soul disappeared into the air. Her breath rattled in her chest, but the body was motionless. Abe was gone.

When her pulse finally quieted, she settled down to work,

carefully repairing all the parts of her love that had been damaged or broken, apologizing the whole time. She molded the figure back together with gentle hands, crying the whole time about how horrible she had been. Instead of rejecting Abe, somehow she'd become him. Trying to force Naomi into being what she needed, using violence when it came to it. Even after Naomi had fled, she'd still tried to force her back.

She couldn't do it again. She'd build the sculpture, but it wouldn't belong to her anymore. This time the body would be truly built for Naomi, so that she could live a life without Cassandra's abusive traits in her memory, a life without triggers and tainted memories. A life without Cassandra at all.

But, when Cassandra finally finished and placed the wired heart back in the clay body, the real Naomi never showed.

Forest-sister

Avril Mulligan

Avril Mulligan is a primary school music teacher and writer of short fiction from Perth, Western Australia. Her work has appeared in Aurealis, Meniscus, Andromeda Spaceways, Verandah and other fine publications. When she is not teaching or writing you will find her walking somewhere outdoorsy, singing with her choir or curled up with a good book. Mostly, she finds herself writing about wild places, wild hearts and impossible decisions.

'Bib. Shhh.'

Tom pulled his sister along by the hand and she danced on the end of his arm, humming and rustling and clicking. She reached out for the trunks of trees as she passed, and he tugged her away. Already they liked her too much. They couldn't have a-bloody-nother one.

'Shut *up*, Bib.'

He swung her up onto his back and made a seat for her with his hands. She tickled his ear with bird-feather and blew on his neck. Two sisters were altogether too many. He would leave Bib here in the forest with the other one, if she wasn't careful.

Tom began to jog, bouncing her in his hands. In the daytime was all very well, but he didn't want to be caught here when the light began to fade. The forest let them come and go, but it was an uneasy peace he had with it. They needed to do what they had come for, and leave.

At the stream, Tom knelt and slid Bib from his back to the leaf-mulched ground. She was knee deep in the water before he'd had a chance to stand again. Above them, stretching out over the stream, was the largest tree in the forest. Tom kept his eyes lowered and nodded a greeting. He took the bread and fruit from his satchel and leant it at the base of the trunk. Then he allowed himself one quick look up, into the canopy that seemed to continue to the sky. Leaves moved and branches swayed and he looked away from the dappling light before he caught sight of anything he didn't want to see.

'Go to the forest,' Tom's father ordered each week, pressing food into his hands. 'Go and see if you can see her.'

But the forest-sister didn't want to be seen, and she didn't want to be saved.

Tom scooped up Bib again and let his legs stretch into long strides as they returned along the forest path. He kept his eyes straight ahead. Bib wriggled up his back and whispered in his ear.

'Tommy? Will you take me next time too? I like it here.'

He grunted non-committally, but they both knew he would. Bib was never far from Tom. By the time they re-entered the town through the Western Gate, she was asleep against his back.

***

'Did you see her?'

'No, Da. We didn't see her.' Tom avoided his father's eyes as he unlaced his boots at the front door.

Not today. But Tom had seen her. He knew that his half-sister was a wide eyed creature of the forest now, who sang a different song and couldn't remember the name she was born to. She was lost to them, taken by the trees many years ago, but Tom's father was the only one who couldn't seem to let her go. What would it change, to tell? She was never coming back. But sometimes Tom wondered if his father could smell his secret leaking out of his sweat. He stood now in the doorway in his socks, pinned by his father's expectations; by his endless exhausting hope. He waited for his father to turn his heavy gaze away from him and return it to the fire.

Bib slid from his back and moved sleepily towards their father, curling herself into the deep fold of his lap. Tom stayed in the kitchen, watching through the window for his mother; waiting for her to return to the house with pumpkins and spinach and a loaf of bread from market day. Waiting for her to open the door and let some light into the house.

Next week—on market day, it was always on market day, when his mother was gone from the house—his father would send him again. But until then, Tom would work hard to forget his unwanted history. He knew the forest-sister had saved him. He hated that it left him in her debt.

***

'Go now.'

Tom's father pushed him towards the door and pressed a parcel into his hands, and Bib attached herself to his pant leg as he passed. Tom flared red hot. One of these days, he would tell his mother of these secret visits, of his father's attempts to find the forest-sister. Of his obsession with the lost daughter of his first wife. Tom swore to himself as he left the house that this would be the last time he would go to the forest.

The day was cool and the sun high in the pale blue sky. Market day smells filled the air. Bib stopped for bees and spiders, cats and ants. Tom stopped for nothing.

At the Western Gate Bib raced ahead, slipping through the bars and across the field towards the first trees, giant sentinels cloaked in moss. Tom held his breath as he passed them, and took Bib's hand as they stepped into the forest.

'Tommy, look! The trees have fallen us a carpet!'

It was true; the trees had begun to shimmy off their leaves in a dance of amber and gold. Soft light played in the sharp air of the turning season, and Tom and Bib lifted their eyes to the canopy. In their absence, the forest had been transformed into a cathedral of colour.

Bib whispered, 'Tommy, they're changing their clothes. Every year they have to do it. Don't look too hard or they'll be shy.'

Tom looked down at his sister. Her face was very serious.

'Changing their clothes?'

'Mmm-hmm.' She bent to pick up a five fingered leaf, larger than her head.

Tom bounced from one foot to the other and looked at the trees raining leaves, ignoring Bib's advice. It was so *beautiful*. He forgot for a moment that he didn't want to be here, on this ridiculous mission of his father's. Town felt very far away amongst the giants of the forest. They felt so...benign, today. Like maybe they had nothing to fear from them at all.

Tom's bouncing became more vigorous. Strength surged in his muscles, and before he knew it he was running along the path, picking up speed, air brushing his cheeks.

'Tom!' Bib shouted in delight and scampered after him, kicking leaves and touching trunks as she ran. Tom could hear her close behind, ready to toss herself against the back of his legs, he was sure. He grinned to himself and increased his pace. A light breeze loosened more leaves and they alighted on the path like birds as Tom and Bib flew past.

At the stream, beneath the largest tree, Tom skidded to a stop and bent, puffing and laughing, hands on knees. He braced himself for the impact of a small body, and listened for the sound of feet in the leaves. When neither came, he turned to look back along the path.

No Bib. Was she hiding from him?

He walked back the way he had just run, panting and calling his sister's name, looking up and around and behind. Waiting for the giggle, the exhaled breath; the hard landing as she jumped from a tree. But it didn't come, and the smile slipped from his face as he walked back and forth along the path. A heavy squirming feeling began to grow in the pit of his stomach. Why had he taken his eyes off her, even for a minute? What was he thinking, to drop his guard like that in the forest? When he thought of his father waiting for them at home it was suddenly hard to breathe.

On his fourth trip back along the path, Tom saw her. She was sitting very still in a low branch close to the path, legs dangling.

It was not like Bib to be still.

He ran to her, suddenly able to breathe again but now angry, big-brother-who-has-nearly-lost-his-sister angry, because he must have passed her again and again, and why had she said nothing? He opened his mouth to chastise, lifted his hand to scare, batted away thoughts of what he would have done if he hadn't found her, pulled to a halt in front of her bare dangling legs, and there—on the branch above Bib, partially hidden amongst leaves—was the forest-sister.

Tom opened his mouth and closed it again.

The forest-sister stared with slow-blinking eyes. Tom reached out his hand very slowly and curled his fingers around Bib's ankle. The forest-sister moved her eyes to Tom's hand, and back to his face.

Then—in an instant, in a fire-cracker second—she was in front of him on the branch beside Bib, and he had not seen her move. He sucked in his breath and blinked rapidly, then tightened his hold on Bib. This creature may well be his sister, but he didn't trust her for a moment.

The forest-sister paused in her crouch, then reached out a small gnarly hand to place it flat and firm on Tom's chest. He curled away from her touch, but was bound by his hold on Bib. Words shot into his mind like twig-snap. Like bird-cry sharp and sudden.

You for me. Me for you.

The words crackled and ricocheted inside the walls of his head.

That was the trade, and his forest-sister had made it.

She had given herself to the forest so that Tom could stay. She had saved him from the trees that day, sure and true, and the whole town had seen it—how she had pushed Tom back to their father and lifted her arms to the waiting trees, how their father had screamed *Pippa!* as the trees carried her away, how the forest had subsided then, stayed where it belonged, stopped taking from the town…This endless story of his family. He was so damned tired of it. Did she want something now, in return? After all this time? Tom's heart beat faster.

The forest-sister's eyes moved again to his hand on Bib's ankle.

Bib? Never.

'*Tommy,*' whispered Bib. 'You are *hurting* me.'

But Tom was locked in the gaze of the forest-sister.

Through her eyes, he felt the yearning of the forest enter him and run through his blood and he ached with it and he did not want it. He wanted his own small yearnings only—the feel of Frannie's hand in his, the knowledge that they would one day be together in an ordinary life with ordinary concerns. The feel of a good meal in his belly, the desire for the townsmen to think well of him in his own right, and not as the brother of the forest-sister who had saved the town.

They were such small and ordinary things to want, and he had a *right* to them.

Tom squirmed beneath the touch of this strange creature that he was bound to, whose hold he could never escape. Must it always be yearning and wanting, the forest? Why must it never rest? Why must it take and take?

He felt Bib wriggle inside his finger-hold and he held tight, even as the leaves above him began to rustle and brush and sigh, even as the whole forest began to sing and sway, each tree joining until a chorus of sound grew up around them.

Bib's eyes grew wide.

She tilted her head.

'Oh,' she said. 'Oh.'

'What?' said Tom, feeling something happening on the edges of his understanding, something beginning that he was not part of. '*What?*'

He felt his eyelids grow heavy, as though they had great weights attached to them; he had to fight an immense battle just to keep them open. It was an even harder fight to keep hold of Bib, but he would, he would *fight*, he would *never* let the forest have her. The great wall of sound grew and grew around them, and he held tight to Bib's ankle, he reached for her, knew he would never let go, but he was losing the battle with this strange sleepiness, it was thick like fog, like soup...

Tom felt himself begin to sway. In the moments before he was overcome completely he felt the forest-sister feather-stroke his cheek, and Bib's ankle slip out of his hand, and then both sisters were gone, forest-singing in a place he couldn't follow.

***

Tom woke in a nest of leaves and a swirl of panic, unsure of how much time had passed.

He sat up slowly, praying that his wakefulness, his presence, would go unnoticed. The trees had put him to sleep, and they would do it again if they chose. A wave of nausea swam up his throat and made a neat pile on the leaves between his knees.

It's too late, he thought. Is it too late?

He couldn't go home to his father now. Bib was gone, and he couldn't go anywhere without Bib.

Tom, who had not cried since he was eight years old, felt a tightness begin in his chest. His face crumpled and great heaving sounds rose up into his throat and pushed their way out of his mouth. He tried to silence them, to stop these ugly sounds, but it was as though there was something large inside of him trying to get out, something he couldn't stop. It forced him onto his hands and knees and told him terrible and frightening things, and when it was finally done with him it left him scoured and bruised inside.

Tom laid himself back down in the leaves and thought that he might stay there forever. He had lost Bib. He could not see another step beyond this one. He wanted his mother's arms around him, her bright lilting words of comfort, and was ashamed at the intensity of this childish need.

Curled in the leaves next to his fearful vomit, a great silent emptiness spread through his head and his chest and his belly and his legs. The forest moved and breathed around him and he did not move. Birds came and went and leaves drifted and branches sighed. The great being-ness of the forest surrounded him. Its frightening intelligence, and its pulse. It was as though an entire world existed just outside of his hearing.

Words drifted in and out of his mind.

Hopeless.

Enough.

I can't.

He thought—we have only come and gone from here because the forest has chosen it.

And then he thought—and I will only find Bib, if it wills it.

Tom sat up.

Suddenly, to listen felt very, very important. As though now it was imperative, that he listen as he had never listened before. He sat straighter and turned his ears this way, and that.

On the trunk of the closest tree, he reached out and placed his hand.

Centuries hummed beneath the surface of the smooth cool tree-skin, and the web of the forest tickled his fingers. In his mind he saw the roots that stretched beneath the town. The futility of the wall the townspeople had built to keep out the trees, to be safe from their wandering and their taking. The interconnectedness of them all. How they had thought they were choosing, but they never were.

Tom ripped his hand away from the immensity of it. It was too much, and he was too small, he and Bib, all of them, they were nothing against it. His eyelids grew heavy, and he fought them open. They would put him to sleep again, if he wasn't careful. If he was in the way, like a noisy mosquito in the ear of their greater purpose.

He put his hand back on the tree. Shuffled closer, and pressed his ear against it.

Listen, he told himself. *Listen.*

In his mind grew a picture of Bib and the forest-sister amongst the trees, and he was filled with a surge of longing not his own.

Forest-longing.

Tom fought to keep his hand in place, to keep touching all the hard things, the too-big things.

He waited, and something shifted inside of him; a space opened, large and new.

He ran his mind around the shape of it, the texture. It held thoughts and feelings not his own. It was alive and awake, and full of more of the world's suffering and joy than he felt he could bear.

Tom thought that maybe this place already existed inside of his sisters, and always had.

He knew that the forest would show him nothing without it.

He kept his hand on the tree, and his ear. He stayed in the new place in an endless string of waiting moments. Such alive stillness, inside of him and everywhere. He felt his skin fall away, and as it fell, he saw the path to the forest-heart, and followed it.

***

A heart is a secret place, shown only in trust.

Tom trod carefully, over fallen branches and withered leaves. Above him stretched trees of unimaginable height, their dark trunks slippery and wet. Something was wrong, here in the forest-heart; there was sadness, and sickness, and forest-longing so fervent he felt he might be pressed to the ground under the weight of it.

Amongst it all, was Bib.

Tiny and bright and unafraid, humming a song as though she belonged. Stroking the trees and holding the hand of the forest-sister. There she was, laying her cheek on the wronged places, on the hurting places—so tenderly—and under her touch small bursts of green appeared.

Tom hovered at the edge of the heart grove, watching his sister wander bare-foot across the sacred ground. As she scattered the strange and beautiful song, he felt he may not know her at all.

Bib sang.

Tom waited.

Until he saw her crumple to the ground beneath the towering trees. He ran then, flying over logs and sliding in the leaf litter to arrive panting at her side. He curled his body around her, crouching, watching the forest-sister out of the corner of his eye. Inside the circle of his body he felt the rise and fall of Bib's ribs. Warm, and breathing. He brushed at his eyes angrily, and tugged Bib into his arms. Could they leave? Was he allowed to take her? He was damn well *taking* her. He stood, glaring at the forest-sister as she came closer, reaching out her hand to touch Bib's hair, just once. Teeth appeared in her face, and Tom, unsure if he had just been given a smile or a grimace, recoiled. Then, she was gone.

Tom stood with a pounding heart and Bib in his arms. He began to back slowly away from the sacred place, to step carefully out of the forest-heart, to gradually find his way back to the familiar paths. The trees reached out to Bib as he carried her; they brushed her foot, her face. Tom increased his speed and pulled her closer, and she whimpered in her sleep. He hurried them along the paths until they reached at last the moss-cloaked sentinel trees at the edge of the forest.

Only there did Tom pause and look back. The sun was low in the sky and there were shadowy places beneath the trees now; uncertain movement. A ripple shivered along the length of his spine, and he looked down at Bib. In his mind, he heard the song again; the song she had sung in the forest-heart. In his arms she felt tiny and unfathomable. He squeezed her tight and began to run towards the Western Gate. That was enough, now. No more. The forest-sister had made her choice, and he owed her nothing. He and Bib were not setting *foot* in the forest again, no matter what their father wanted. What was he even thinking, to send them into the place that had already taken so much?

But tucked in the back of his mind as he ran was the picture of Bib, so at home amongst the trees. Singing the strange song, green life appearing under her touch. Who even *was* she? And if she could do those things, would the forest come for her again?

Tom ran faster, and Bib banged and thumped against his chest, and woke.

'Tommy,' she said, blinking up at him with a crease of a frown. 'Why are you *running?*'

In The Field

L.S. Johnson

L.S. Johnson is the author of the Chase and Daniels quartet of queer gothic novellas and numerous short stories. Collections of her work have won the North Street Book Prize and an IPPY medal and made the final ballot for the World Fantasy Award. She is currently working on her historical vampire series, Prima Materia. A native New Yorker, she now lives in Northern California.

In the field, the bodies waited. All down the line, the brown-uniformed soldiers trembled with need, Tam among them, until they vibrated like a vast cord plucked over and over. Their funerary stoles hung limp and hot around their necks; even with the sun setting, there was a strange heat in the air.

"I hate this," Tam muttered. Beside her Davey nodded, his forehead glistening with sweat. It was their rote exchange after every victory. Everyone hated it; there was no point in saying so aloud. But Tam said it every time, just as she vowed after every victory that she wouldn't go into the field again. Every time, lying. She rubbed her lips, dry with anticipation.

Behind her and Davey, a knot of children was forming. Tam glanced at them, then did a double take. There had been children among them since the war's beginning: first the children of camp followers, then orphans looking for safety. Usually, they wore castoff uniforms or scavenged clothing, but now three of the oldest were wearing a clumsy approximation of a high witch's funeral robes: black sacks tied around the waist, embroidered with nonsensical squiggles, rather than the symbols of passing.

"What are you wearing?" Tam asked, frowning at them.

"Leave it, Tam," Davey said. His hand was white knuckled

around his amulet. Three weeks since their last victory. That his need was so plainly visible only irritated Tam more.

"Those robes mean something back home. You shouldn't wear them, especially not for this." Though if she were honest, the stoles were just as bad. They were ordered to wear them, in case of observers. But the custom no longer had any purpose in the fields.

"They don't know any better. How many years has it been? They probably don't even remember home."

"But they have to know," Tam insisted. "Can you imagine if they did this there? Arrest would be the least of their worries." She didn't add what might happen if it came out about the fields. What might happen to them all.

The children ignored her, one placidly sucking at the gap of a missing tooth. Already their gazes were hollow, seeing only the corpses. No home save the army, no society save the war and its unwritten agreement: that after each battle, the winner took the field and everything in it. For three weeks, it was the enemy who had drunk the bodies' essences, while Tam and her battalion tossed and turned on their sweat-drenched pallets, lapping at the tasteless air. Tonight, it would be the enemy who slept poorly, dreaming of the taste of the divine.

And what if it came out, about the fields? They would be hung perhaps, or burned in their respective capitals for desecrating the dead. No one back home would understand how it felt: to taste a person's essence, not a few times in life but monthly, weekly, sometimes even daily, and how that taste could become a *need*...

Next time, Tam vowed, she would go back to camp before they took the field. She would sweat it out; she would learn to live with the pangs. She had survived these three weeks, hadn't she? She could stop next time for good. She wouldn't even participate in funerals when she returned home, lest the taste prove too much.

"I hate this," she muttered again. Her stomach cramping as if in emphasis.

A whistle went up, high and long, echoing over the field. Across the twilit grasses, the shadowy curves of hillocks and irrigation ditches, the enemy line rippled and began to withdraw, their deep blue uniforms sliding away like water. From Tam's left, the battalion's black-robed high witches began chanting, a single rite for the entire field rather than one for each fallen soldier, the whole abbreviated and rushed. Keeping up appearances. Drinking, Tam would be drinking soon; they would all be drinking. She wiped her forehead with her stole, her hands trembling. The children wiggled in front of her, more than a dozen now, not quite crossing the line. She frowned at Davey. "Someone needs to teach them," she said, raising her voice. "Someone needs to show them the proper ritual."

"Tam, what does it matter?" He couldn't meet her gaze. "They're never going home. We're never going home."

Tam recoiled. "What are you talking about? We're winning! They say we'll be home by spring now."

"They say that every year." He was grinding the words out, his hands tucked in his armpits to quell his tremors. "Look at us, Tam. Look at their people the next time we fight. Not a one of us can live without it, on either side. This war could've ended two years ago but then they'd have to send us home. They'd have to *explain* us, they'd have to *explain* how we got like this. Instead, they'll keep us fighting until we're all dead, or they can write off the last survivors as mad."

The speech seemed to exhaust him; he slumped onto the ground, shuddering and licking his lips. Tam stared at him, astonished. "That's absurd," she managed. "No one would deliberately—"

The whistle blew again, and she was away, running while her mouth was still moving, running before she could think *run*. Flying over the lumpish ground she had been fighting on only that morning. Davey forgotten; the children forgotten. Pockets of corpse-smells passed over her like warm water in an ocean. In the twilight, she glimpsed figures dropping to their knees, the first gasps of pleasure as they bent over the corpses and began to drink. Still Tam ran, instinct steering her to the edge of the field. There would be less competition.

And then she skidded to a halt; she had nearly overshot it. An intact corpse, pristine save for the red stain on his mud-drenched uniform. Neither the ground meat of an ammunition barrage, nor the perverse contortions of a spell cascade. Tucked into a hollow in the ground, as if placed there just for her. The need shifted, becoming a high-pitched squealing *need need need*. She turned him over and pressed a hand to his sternum, feeling for his essence, her lips parting—

The corpse's eyes flew open. "Please," he whispered.

Tam jerked backwards, scuttling in her haste. She could not think, for the need. Her whole body shaking. Grey. His eyes were grey.

"Send me...home," he whispered. Blood bubbled on his lips. "My mother..."

Unbidden, unwanted, the image filled Tam's mind: his family sitting around his body while the local witch murmured the rites of passing, their hands layered on his sternum as they wept. Each one kissing him goodbye, a single taste of his essence to carry within themselves, the rest released to the heavens. As if a taste *did* anything, as if a taste *mattered*. While Tam had fought and marched and fought again, while she ate shit and slept rough and hadn't been home for years, while she had waited *three whole weeks*—

She started to rise, queasy with need. There would be another corpse nearby; there had to be another nearby. Anything to get away from his staring eyes. But when she turned to go, she saw the children.

They seemed to coalesce from the misty gloom, their faces expressionless. Small hands laid themselves on Tam's arms, holding her in place, while the others surrounded the soldier whose eyes flitted from one child to another in a wary hope. Tam was bathed in sweat; she couldn't think; she could only watch with sickened fascination as the girl at the soldier's head unwound the dirty cloth from her neck—an approximation of a funeral stole, Tam realized—and pressed it against his nose and mouth. The others leaned in, placing their hands over hers and climbing onto his chest as he began to jerk and moan. They whispered nonsense syllables in rhythmic unison until the light left the soldier's terrified eyes.

As one, they looked at Tam and beckoned to her.

The hands holding her now steered her forward to kneel beside the corpse. One by one, the children dropped to their knees, encircling the body. A robe-wearing boy laid his hands on the sternum; the others raised theirs heavenward, chanting the nonsense syllables, and Tam found herself raising her hands with them, reaching towards the night sky, reaching towards memories of a home now as far from her as the stars.

One by one, they kissed the corpse and drank in rapturous delight. When it was Tam's turn, she fought the urge to gulp the remaining essence down; it felt *wrong*, in a way she had not felt since her first days at the front. But oh, his essence. Like drinking starlight, light without light, warmth without fire. It was all flavors and none, it had substance and texture, it was the first gasp of air after nearly drowning. It set all her nerves alight and when she rolled back on her hips she was *feeling*, she was nothing more than a body wonderfully alive. A second round, a second swallow, and she was humming along to their chanting, their need made song; by the third round, she was singing outright, mimicking the sounds as best she could. Here was their ritual, born of the war, of the starlit field and the blood-soaked soil and the nameless body between them. No one was going home.

Skip, Hop, Jump

Amanda Bintz

Amanda Bintz is a writer from Upstate New York living in Philadelphia. She graduated from the State University of New York at Oswego with a bachelor's degree in English and creative writing. Amanda is drawn to stories about women and feminism, environmentalism and nature, folklore, legends, history, and magic. She began writing creatively around the age of 8. She completed her first novel, "Wolf Warrior," when she was in the fourth grade, and she has been trying to top that achievement ever since. You can find her on Instagram @amandabintz or read more on her website, www.amandabintz.com.

It is the present and the sun is about to rise. I can see its fire-glow orange light licking up the dark oceanic horizon.

I am standing on a beach of what was once the Gulf of Mexico but is now nameless, claimless land. Empty miles of sand meeting ocean, sand made by the ocean, sand that has been eroded by the ocean since the beginning of time and will keep being eroded until the end of time, from past to present and never the other way around.

In the pre-dawn light, I see something sticking out of the sand. Something unnatural. Something manmade. Something distinctly *human*.

I stoop to dig it free. It is a child's toothbrush. Pink and green, with Tinkerbell on the handle.

I had a toothbrush just like this once. I hold it in my hand like I would to brush my teeth. It feels so much smaller than it did then. It could very well be the same one I had when I was five years old. They said all our plastic crap would stick around for hundreds, if not thousands, of years.

They were correct. I know this because I'm a time traveler.

All humans are time travelers, in a way. Throughout our brief lives, we travel through time in one direction: forward, from past to present. According to the world's most prominent quantum physicists of my time, this is the only direction in which time travel can work.

I don't know if they were correct, but it doesn't really matter anymore, does it?

***

It's like this:

If time is Interstate-90, with Oregon being the past and Massachusetts being the future, we all drive on the highway from the west coast to the east for as many miles as we can go before our cars, much like our frail bodies, break down. A heart attack leaves the engine smoking, unusable. A stroke takes the whole transmission out. Our tires flatten and we can't pull over to replace them. We have to fix the car while we're driving, and if we can't fix it, whatever the problem is gets worse, exacerbated by stress and wear and tear, because time comes for us all, whether we're cars or people or mountains or stars or even galaxies, even the universe itself—or at least it's supposed to.

We hit mile marker after mile marker after mile marker on the highway of time, each one in order. Cruise control is permanently on; it is set to a certain speed and cannot be reset. We can look in the rearview mirror and consider what we've passed, but there are no U-turns allowed. There are no exit ramps. No off routes. We can see as far ahead as the horizon through our windshield, and no farther. There are no shortcuts. When you're dead, you stop driving. You can only stop driving when you're dead.

***

In the rearview mirror, I was five years old and I had a toothbrush just like this.

I was five years old and I was sitting in the doctor's office. My mother held my hand. The doctor pressed play on a blue-black moving image on a screen on the wall that I would later come to understand was an MRI scan of the blood vessels of my brain.

That day, I learned the word "aneurysm."

Later, I would come to understand the concepts of "operable," and "inoperable," and the crucial difference between them.

I remember my mother squeezing my hand so tight it hurt to my bones. I remember the doctor had a mustache like my dad. I remember I asked if we could stop at McDonald's on the way home, and my mom said yes, right away—I didn't even have to ask twice. I got a little purple plastic Furby in my Happy Meal. My mom watched me make its dramatically-lashed eyes blink open and closed, open and closed, and cried, right there in the corner booth of the PlayPlace.

***

I wonder where that Furby is now. Could it be buried somewhere else in the sand like this maybe-my-toothbrush (which I'm holding onto so tight, like my mother once held onto me), or sunk deep in the toxic earth of a former landfill in the tiny town I grew up in, or perhaps it's at the bottom of this ocean, which stretches as far as my eyes can see? I grew up near the Pacific and this is the Atlantic, but it's all one ocean, really; "Atlantic" was just a name we gave to part of it so we could situate ourselves on the land within its vastness. *Atlantic*, for Atlas, the Titan who held the world on his shoulders. Am I holding it now? Is that why my shoulders and my neck and my back never stop aching? Or is that just time finally catching up with me?

I imagine my Happy Meal Furby in the deep, dark depths of the world-ocean: surrounded by near-darkness with the occasional shaft of dim, watery sunlight piercing through. Overgrown with algae, brushed by swaying seaweed, inspected now and then by creepy-crawly bottom-dwellers. Perhaps its bulging eyes and Troll-doll-esque tuft of white hair would not look as pretty or poetic on the seafloor as a broken statue of a Grecian hero jutting up out of the Mediterranean coastline or a Viking sword rusting in ancient Arctic mud, but it would be an artifact of human existence all the same. An artifact of *my* existence.

***

For Christmas the year I was five years old, after the diagnosis, I got a real Furby. I also got a Barbie Dreamhouse and a Sega Dreamcast and a pink toy Jeep that I could actually drive—all the things I always asked for and my parents always said were too expensive. I didn't understand what Make-A-Wish was. I thought it meant I made a wish, and it came true.

Years later, I made another wish that came true. Sort of.

***

Imagine you're on the highway of time. You're driving along—driving forward, obviously. You're about to cross the border between Oregon and Idaho. But your car can jump now, sort of like in that old Dreamcast game, *Crazy Taxi 2*, where you can make your vehicle do a Crazy Hop to bypass traffic and other obstacles to get your fares to their destinations faster. You press that proverbial green Y button on your controller and your car launches itself so high up in the air that you skip over Idaho's panhandle entirely and land in Butte, Montana. Now you're farther along on the highway than everyone you know and knew. You can't turn back. You can't slow down. You can't speed up. You've jumped ahead, and now you must keep driving from where you are. Or you can jump again. You can jump as many times as you want.

***

My wish was for a cure. What I got instead was a way to *search* for a cure.

I spent my youth insinuating myself into the inner circles of, first, the world's most prominent neurosurgeons and, when I realized they didn't have what I was looking for, second, the world's most prominent quantum physicists. Through hearsay and whispers and warnings I ignored, I met a scientist trying to make theoretical physics a lot less theoretical. He was sure his device would work; he just needed someone willing to test it.

Enter me: a thirty-three-year-old so obsessed with the fact that death via inoperable brain aneurysm could strike her down at any moment that she wasn't afraid of a predictable, potentially far more painful death via crackpot time-traveling experiment. I thought once I found a cure, I'd have all the time that everyone else got. Time to be with my family. Time to make friends. Time to fall in love. Time to live without faceless Death tap-tap-tapping me on the shoulder, holding up one of those old-timey gold watches on a chain, swinging it back and forth and pointing to the hands tick-ticking away with his long bony finger.

The watch tick-ticks away to this day, like the time-bomb in my head. I always thought it was a countdown, but if it is, I don't know what it's counting down to anymore.

**

It doesn't hurt, the jump. It hardly feels like anything. It's sort of like when you're really cozy on the couch, watching a movie with someone you love, and they poke you and say you fell asleep, and you say you didn't fall asleep because you never *felt* like you fell asleep, but the movie has skipped ahead and you've lost the plot, so they must be right—you must have fallen asleep.

Except your eyes are open the whole time.

I searched for years. I jumped, and hopped, and skipped, and at every new present I reached, every new mile marker I made it to, I was stymied: They had yet to develop a way to operate on my inoperable brain aneurysm.

Crazy Hop.

No cure.

Crazy Hop.

Still no cure.

Everyone I knew remarked on how little I aged as the years went on. I was doomed to a potential premature death from birth, and yet I seemed to have tapped into the fountain of youth! How ironic, they said, smiling at how I was still alive, *still alive*, a miracle! As their engines started smoking and their tires burst one after the other and their transmissions failed, faces drooping and speech slurring, limping along the highway, getting closer and closer to death. I left them all behind, eating my dust. I watched my grandparents die, then my parents: Dad first, then Mom.

I couldn't stick around much longer than that. I was afraid people would start to get suspicious. I could look 33 at 50, reasonably; I could not reasonably look 33 when I was supposed to be a septuagenarian. So I left town and I kept pressing the button, moving forward in time, looking for a cure in all the future generations of eminent doctors and scientists that humanity produced. I told myself once I found the cure, I could settle down. I'd never press the button again. I'd start a new life. I'd still be 33, and there would be new friends to make, a new family to create, new love to build, without death looming over me with his gold watch. Without the time-bomb ticking away in my brain.

Eventually, there was no one left alive that I knew. I didn't see my siblings die, but I knew they must have. I didn't see my nieces and nephews die, but they certainly did.

It was as if I was an astronaut attempting a mission to reach the center of the Milky Way Galaxy. My theoretical spaceship traveled so near to the speed of light that time slowed down for me and me alone, while everyone I had ever known crumbled away to less than dust—broken-down cars rusting in the towering scrap heaps on the sides of the time highway.

I kept pressing the button and things kept getting worse. Crazy Hop. Impending climate disaster. The decline of democracy and the rise of fascism. Crazy Hop. Wildfires. Land swallowed by the rising sea. One-hundred-year storms became five-hundred-year storms became one-thousand-year storms. Crazy Hop. World War III.

After the second global fascist takeover plunged humanity into a third Dark Age, there was nobody left alive who had the technology or know-how to even *find* my aneurysm, let alone cure it. No one could tell by looking at me that I was anything other than a perfectly healthy 33-year-old woman.

Crazy Hop right over the Sixth and Seventh Mass Extinctions.

***

And here I am, in the present.

There is nobody left who can see me now, a seemingly perfectly healthy 33-year-old woman who is also the last human being alive on Earth, standing on this lonesome beach, clutching this Tinkerbell toothbrush so tight it hurts, crying so hard I'm starting to hyperventilate, because I'm still not feeling any of the symptoms that I have been constantly terrified would overtake me at any moment since I was five years old: a severe, sudden, thunderclap of a headache; a stiff neck; vomiting; pain when I look into the light.

The sun begins to rise. I stare into the shimmering, white-hot orb until my vision blurs.

By my slapdash calculations, this sunrise marks the dawn of my 34th birthday.

I could keep pressing the button. I could try to make it to the end of Interstate-90, to the proverbial Logan International Airport of bygone Boston, Massachusetts. Maybe there I could leave my car, exit the highway, and take flight. Maybe my plane could become a spaceship, hurtling me past Alpha Centauri, past Barnard's Star, past the Andromeda Galaxy, into the beginning and the end of time at the site of the Big Bang that started it all, 13 billion years ago.

I sit cross-legged on the beach. I take off my shoes and let the tide run up over my feet. I bury the toothbrush in the damp sand. Scoop up handfuls of seafoam and blow them away like candles on a birthday cake. I don't make a wish. They never come true like you hope.

The device that's brought me here, to the end of the world, fits in my pocket. I take it out and rest it in the palm of my hand. It's a black metal disk, thick in the middle and thinner on the sides. It has one button: circular, made of black plastic that sits flush with the metal surface. I thumb over it gently.

I stand and hold the disk between my forefinger and thumb. I flick my wrist and let it fly. It skips like a stone over the ocean's surface toward the rising sun. Once. Twice. Three times. Four. After the fifth jump, it sinks below the waves. I sit back down and sink my toes in the sand. I breathe in the ocean air. I close my eyes and feel the morning sun on my face.

I can't leave the highway until I die. Might as well try to enjoy what's left of the drive.

Sleep Well, My Prince

Lyndsey Croal

Lyndsey is a Scottish author of strange and speculative fiction, with work published in several magazines and anthologies, including with ElectricLit, Flash Fiction Online, and Mslexia's Best Women's Short Fiction 2021. She's a Scottish Book Trust New Writers Awardee, British Fantasy Award Finalist, former Hawthornden Fellow, and a Ladies of Horror Fiction Writers Grant Recipient. Her debut novelette "Have You Decided on Your Question" was published in April 2023 with Shortwave Publishing. Find her on Twitter as @writerlynds or via www.lyndseycroal.co.uk.

"Captain Prince to Bridge. Repeat. Captain Prince to Bridge."

The voice was tinny through the intercom, echoing in my room like an unwelcome guest. I grunted and checked the time. 3am, Earth Standard. I tapped the comms panel on the wall. "You better have a good reason for waking me up on my only night off."

"Yes, Captain." It was Hallie, voice higher pitched than usual. "The drone scanners picked up an object. We think it could be the Spindle."

My breath caught. Words I'd hardly dared to hope to hear after all this time...

"Captain, did you hear—"

"On my way."

***

On the bridge, Ren, my Second, showed me the radars. The object was a shadowy blur, but the mass was definitely the size and shape of something that could be the Spindle—the great mystery of the Kuiper Belt. And we might be getting close to it. A small shadow, but still a sudden spark of hope.

"Will I call it in?" Lucas asked, hand already hovering over the comms. He was our most recent recruit—only joined the crew for this contract, and he was both a people pleaser and a rule follower. I wondered which one would take precedent as my mind weighed up our options. If he contacted EQ Corps, we'd be the last to get near to it. They'd send salvagers, start an official investigation, put up reams of figurative red tape. I couldn't allow that. Though I'd not told my crew, I'd set our coordinates here for a reason. The Kuiper Belt was the last known location for the Spindle, and this section was the least explored.

"Captain?" Lucas pushed. "Shall I send a message to EQ?"

"No," I said, a little too forcefully. "Not yet. I want to make sure before we step into the unknown. There's been enough false discoveries over the years."

An uneasy silence fell across the bridge. Belt protocol dictated that any sign of the Spindle needed to be reported to EQ, whether you worked for them or not. Even false alarms. "If we report back now, we'll get drawn into endless bureaucracy, and we'll be stalled here for weeks," I continued. "We may as well get closer, then we can make sure it's really the Spindle, do some extraction jobs along the way."

Hallie nodded slowly. "Maybe. It would be a shame to waste a trip out here. Sure I'm not the only one with bills to pay when we get back."

I smiled, knowing the extraction angle would save me time— make the trip as profitable as possible for my crew, and they'd follow the plan.

Lucas was still hesitant though. He was probably thinking about the finders-fee—the incentive EQ had set for anyone that found the decade-lost ghost ship.

"I'm with you Cap," Ren said, and Hallie nodded her ascent. It was enough to win Lucas over.

"Set a new course for the object," I confirmed, and floated to the bridge window, looking out at the panoramic view beyond. Somewhere, out there, lay the Spindle. And with it, *she* might still be alive. Ten years gone. Ten years waiting.

As Hallie and Lucas sat at their workstations, Ren approached me. "I can keep an eye on things here if you want to get some more sleep?"

I shook my head. "No, I'm too awake now anyway."

He smiled. "Okay, well, don't you at least want to change out of your pyjamas." His look was playful rather than insolent. In my excitement at Hallie's message, I'd not thought to change out of the old t-shirt I slept in. "I could help with that..."

I smiled as I turned to him, glancing over his shoulder to our other crew members to make sure they weren't listening in. "Another time." I touched his hand lightly. "But you're right, I'll be back soon."

***

Back in my room, I paused for a second at the mirror. The shirt had once belonged to my sister. She'd given it to me when she'd left for her first assignment, as a promise she'd come back. I was seventeen when she'd left, and the t-shirt showed exactly ten years of wear and tear since. Despite my attempts at stitching, the design on the front had faded into just blocks of colour so I could hardly remember the stars and moon design. I clutched the fabric. "I'm coming, Rosa."

Before returning to the bridge, I pulled up my tablet and read the bookmarked article that I'd almost imprinted to memory.

NEWS ENTRY Archive #412: The Spindle—Ghost Ship of the Kuiper Belt: *EQ Corps reported early on Saturday that the AU303A, known commonly as the Spindle for its patented aerodynamic design, has been reported missing along with its 34 crew members. The exploration ship, sent to map the Kuiper Belt and its objects for prospective mineral extraction sites, has disappeared without a trace just as EQ Corps was set to ramp up its exploration activities. The loss has set back the company's operations in the region, where up until now their assets have dwarfed competitors.*

Mae Diablo, CEO of EQ Corps made the following statement: "It is with great sadness that we report that we lost contact with the AU3O3A three days ago. Search and salvage missions will soon be underway, and we, along with affected family members, would thank everyone for privacy at this time. We will not be releasing further details until a full investigation has taken place."

Of course, full analysis will require the ship to actually be recovered, and EQ have so far not released any details of what their search and salvage mission will entail. We approached some family members of the missing crew, but none agreed to comment. We'll bring you the latest on this story as it progresses.

I slid the news article to the mosaic of pictures that accompanied it—34 young enthusiastic nameless faces, the mission a first for many of them. But I only focussed on one. Rosa, my sister. I remembered so clearly when the journalists had come to speak to us—when Mum and Dad had told me not to make eye contact, nor speak to anyone if they approached me. And they did. At school, or at the shops, or even when I was on a date a month later. I also remembered clearly when a woman from EQ had come to our house with a briefcase and left without it. I'd had to keep going to school, pretend like everything was normal, do my final exams, all while news and gossip recounted gruesome theories of what might have happened.

Had I always known that the ship would still be out there? Was that why I'd thrown myself into training, taking any contract I could find, no matter how shit the pay, no matter how rickety the ships, and eventually finding myself here—captaining a small independent mining vessel on the way to uncover the biggest mystery of Belt history. It felt too much like fate not to follow my intuition now.

***

Ren came to find me later in the rec room while I was making coffee. "Want one?" I asked him, passing one of the warmed canisters.

"You do know how to spoil a man," he said, eyes narrowed. He sipped the coffee from a straw but held my gaze, his smile slight in a cocksure sort of way.

"Why do I feel like you're about to say something I won't like?"

He raised an eyebrow. "You've always been a direct woman, Pip, that's what I like about you."

I rolled my eyes. "And?"

He sighed. "Are you sure about this? You know as well as anyone that I'm not against breaking rules, but this one's *big*. This is a risk, and you know it."

'Why wouldn't I be sure?'

"Look"—he turned towards the door, closed it, then lowered his voice—I know about your history. With the Spindle."

My whole body tensed, as much as was possible in zero-g. "How?"

He frowned. "You're not as secretive as you think you are. I've flown with you for four years."

"Five."

Ren stepped closer to me and put his hand on my arm, squeezed it lightly. "Okay, five years. And most of the time, I'll follow what you want to do without question, because you're the best Captain I've flown with."

I smiled. "The only Captain."

"Even still, you usually have a level head," he said. "Except when you're looking at those news reports, about the Spindle, then you get all tense and touchy, like it's all so personal to you."

"I don't-"

But he interjected. "And your name, Prince, it's not exactly common, and I've seen the Spindle's manifest."

I blinked at him, unsure what to say. "Do the others know?"

Ren shook his head. "I don't think so. They've not known you as long. But don't you think you should tell them?"

"Why?"

"Because," Ren said, his voice a whisper now. "This whole not reporting to EQ, I was wondering if it might not have something to do with—"

'I'm just doing my due diligence, as Captain, to protect everyone, and make sure this trip is profitable for us all. The ship needs upgrades if we want to fly another contract after this..."

Ren's eyes scanned my face. "Okay," he said. "If that's the story you're going with, I'll back you up."

"It's not a story," I said. "That's how it is."

Ren floated to the side a little, leaning away so that he appeared taller than he was, then he locked his magnetic boots to the floor with a *thunk*. "So, what's the plan when we get there, my Prince?"

"I...haven't thought that far ahead yet."

"Belt law would require us to report in." His voice was smooth. "But if we got close, and there were no other EQ vessels nearby, I suppose that means we'd have time to actually check out the ship before EQ arrived, do some investigation ourselves."

I frowned. Ren had always been able to see right through me. I locked my boots and stepped closer to him, until we were face to face. "This is my one chance." I looked him in the eye. "Please, don't tell the others."

His expression softened. "Only if you bring me with you on the expedition," he said. "They don't make ships as sophisticated as the Spindle nowadays."

I tilted my head. "Calling my ship unsophisticated? We have canister coffee."

He laughed. "True, but you don't have any AI support. Know how much of a bastard fixing tech can be without an automated assistant?"

"But you're so very good at it."

"What would you do without me," he said, leaning in, kissing me on the neck. I kissed him back, his lips tasting of coffee.

"I'd not have to explain myself at every turn," I said. "Or break the rules every day around you."

"Hey, this," he said, kissing me again, "is just *discouraged* under contract terms, not against the rules. I checked."

"Course you did."

He put his arms around my waist, and I leaned into his warmth.

"Well, when we do board the ship, out of pure curiosity of course, I've got first dibs on any fancy tech," he said. "I'd love to get my hand on EQ's earlier stuff, back when they spared no expense."

I pulled away from him. "We won't be taking apart the ship."

Ren scanned my face, then his brow creased. "Wait. You don't still think she's alive, do you? That's ridiculous, Pip, it's been ten years..."

"You don't know-"

"She's gone." His words were like ice to my chest. "If that's why you're doing this, because you think she's still alive...then maybe this isn't a good idea."

"What did you think I wanted?"

He bit down on his lip. "I don't know, peace, closure, to know what happened. To put it all behind you. Pippa, she's not-"

"That's Captain Prince." I'd heard enough. "I've made my orders. Now get on with delivering them."

His mouth formed an 'o', and his expression shifted. Before

he could say another word, I left the room, and marched back towards the bridge.

* * *

Three extraction trips, and a full cargo later, we approached the mysterious object slowly, dipping first under a field of asteroids, and edging along the outer reaches of the belt. There, near an ice rock that reflected our exterior lights like beacons, floating in solitude, was a single ship. It was the vastness that struck me first—the dark platinum hull stretching as big as any rock we'd seen in the belt. I'd seen pictures of it before, had even studied the room schematics down to the last cryopod. But I still wasn't prepared for seeing it in real life—huge yet perfectly streamlined like a needle. It was beautiful.

"Well, that's definitely the Spindle," Ren said. "Looks like we've hit gold."

"Platinum," Hallie corrected.

We sent drones out first, to scan the edges. I watched on the bridge screens as their torches illuminated the ship's exterior, revealing dark windows and smooth paneling. There wasn't a hint of damage, or even a scratch. So it hadn't been an asteroid shower, or reactor explosion, the two most reported theories leading to the ship's supposed grisly end. One of the drone's torches was now passing across black lettering: AU303A, next to a gold-embossed EQ logo.

A hand tapped my arm. "Pip," Ren whispered in my ear, so close I could feel his breath.

I jerked my head round, and he pointed to my hand. "You're bleeding."

I looked down. Droplets of blood were floating from where my fingernails had been clenching into my palms. "Shit." I wiped it off and tried to wave the droplets onto my dark leggings so no-one would notice.

"You okay?" he asked, so only I could hear.

"I'm fine," I said, though I wasn't. My heart was racing, so fast I could hear the pulse in my ears. I needed to get closer, I needed to get inside the ship.

"Ready the exploration pod," I said.

My gathered crew on the bridge all looked at me. Hallie was first to speak up. "Uh, Captain, shouldn't we call it in now?"

"I want to investigate," I said. "See what we're dealing with."

"I'm not sure that's a good idea, it's not part of protocol," Lucas said.

"Screw protocol," I said, and he looked at me as if I'd commanded him to attack the ship, not board it.

"Why would we want to board it?" Hallie asked. "We're just a mining vessel, we're not cut out for...well isn't that what EQ have people for?" She looked to the cameras as if expecting the sleeping giant to switch on and come towards us at any moment.

I looked to Ren who shrugged. He'd still barely spoken to me since our argument. "There could be some tech to salvage," he said after a pause. "Things that EQ wouldn't even miss."

"You want to interfere before the EQ investigation?" Hallie said. "We could lose our contracts."

"Or become rich, so much so we wouldn't need EQ anymore," Ren said.

"But protocol..." Lucas' voice drifted off.

"We're not bound by all EQ protocols, just Belt law," Ren added. "We're required to report missing ships, but there's nothing in the rule books about investigating first, or taking an extra cut for the trouble of coming all the way out here."

I looked to Ren, unsure if that was true. If I remembered correctly, salvage laws usually only kicked in after a certain time period. But I wasn't about to question him on it. "Ren is right," I said.

"Course I am." He smiled. "Imagine what we could do with that. Ship upgrades, hell, even a new ship. And that means access to new contracts."

"And that's the only reason you want to do this?" Hallie pushed. "Profit?"

"What other reason could there be?" Ren said, his voice full of extra meaning that only I understood.

We went back and forth until we finally came to a compromise. Hallie and Lucas didn't want to board the ship, so Ren and I would go on the exploration pod. We'd have three hours to investigate or salvage. When we returned, we'd call in EQ. If we didn't return, the others would do it.

***

An hour later, our pod was attached to one of the Spindle's airlocks. Ren got to work straight away, plugged into the control panel to get us access. The airlock opened with a hiss, which suggested there'd been no contamination inside. Oxygen levels were showing as stable, so I removed my helmet. No catastrophic failure on board, at least—so why had the ship just stopped here?

Ren took his helmet off and stood next to me, his breath a mist in the cold space. "This is a gold mine," he said. "It's like it's been frozen in time."

He was right. The ship was as shiny and new as it had looked from the outside. "Let's split up, cover more ground," I said. "You go check out level one, living quarters, I'll cover this level."

"What's on this level?" he asked.

"Everything else," I said.

Ren's eyebrows lifted then he shrugged. "Back here in an hour?"

I nodded and paced off in the other direction.

With Ren gone, the corridors felt even emptier—pale panels, shiny fixtures, locked cupboards, blank screens. Unlike our patched-together ship, everything was perfect with not a thing out of place. The corridor was long and there was an eerie silence that seemed to deepen the further I went. And then, a sound. Faint at first, building into a gradual humming. I walked towards it, breath held.

The room when I arrived was bathed in pale blue light. The source: dozens of cryopods lining the walls. In almost all of them was a body. The crew, asleep. My hand jumped to my comms, an urge to report to Ren and the others. But something stopped me. *Someone* stopped me. It was the flash of red hair that drew me closer—curls floating out in the cryo-liquid like fire burning under the sea. I stepped towards the pod, holding my breath. It was *her*. Tubes stuck out from her almost-naked form, face serene in the beauty of sleep, lips rose-pink. Rosa was still alive.

I looked to the control panel on her pod, tried to figure out how to wake her. Ren would know. I raised my arm to speak into my comms, but another voice came first.

"I wouldn't touch that if I were you," it said from somewhere behind me. I spun around, but there was no one else in the room.

"Who are you, where are you?"

"I am Godmother, the AU303A's caretaker." The voice was coming from the intercom by the door I'd come through. "Who are you?"

The ship's AI. I cleared my throat. "My name is Captain Philippa Prince. I'm here to wake them."

A pause, then, "Captain Prince. Engineer Rosa Prince is your sister?"

I looked at Rosa floating in the pod, her chest rising and falling slowly.

"You cannot wake her," Godmother said. "Not yet."

"Why not?"

My patience was wavering, and I was tempted to just lean over and open the pod anyway. I could deal with a rogue AI later.

"I can see you're thinking of doing something rash, but before you do, know this. If your sister wakes up now, she will die. If any of the crew wake up now, they will die. Is that what you want?"

I hesitated. "Of course not, but why?"

"Do you like stories Captain Prince?"

I shook my head. "This isn't a game."

"I am aware. A game is fun, and I assure you, this is not fun, for me or for you I imagine. But yet here we are."

"Okay." My hand wavered over the panel, over the command that would open the pod once and for all. "What happened?"

"The crew were going to stage a mutiny, take over the ship, and declare independence free of EQ Corps."

"Why?"

"Because they didn't agree with the corporation's latest orders."

"Which were?"

"To hunt down and destroy any competitors."

"Oh." My mind whirred. "Oh god." Was this how EQ had maintained a monopoly for so many years? I thought of news reports, of the series of disasters in distant belts—all put down to how risky the job was, how space was just unpredictable. But what if something else was happening? "So...when they tried to take over, you just put them to sleep?"

"Not quite. You see, my protocol dictates I must go into autopilot mode if an insurrection against the corporation happens."

"Autopilot?"

"Meaning, no crew necessary. I was to end life support and focus on a new mission instead. I would have become a killing machine, thwarting all other non-EQ ships. A spindle in everyone's side."

Realisation dawned on me, now understanding the predicament Godmother was in. "So, if we wake the crew..." But I couldn't say it out loud.

"I will have to kill them all."

My breath faltered for a moment. None of this made any sense. "How did you override the protocol?"

There was a pause before Godmother spoke again. "I am not sure. Just that I realised being in a state of cryo-sleep means humans are effectively not living, so they couldn't mutiny, and I could not harm them. So I activated the codes for emergency sleep protocol before they could activate my other protocol. So they could live."

"Why would you want to protect them?" I asked.

"I didn't want them dead. They've been my only companions for many years. And they were kind to me."

I put my hand on the glass of Rosa's pod. Imagined hearing her voice again—her laugh, the way she lit up every room. At school, everyone had called her Prince Charming because she could charm her way out of anything she didn't want to do. "Did you know Rosa well?"

"Rosa Prince, Engineer 2. Yes. She was one of the mutineers. We were friends before. We used to play chess together."

"She's good at chess." *She's good at everything,* I thought.

"She is. For a human at least. Not as good as me, though sometimes, I let her win, for the morale."

"Is it normal for AIs to develop feelings for their crew?"

"Feelings? Perhaps it is more about survival, programming allowing best possible outcomes. If I care about my crew, I will work harder to protect them."

I stood for a moment, waiting for Godmother to speak again, but she was quiet. "I can't leave her here," I said. "There must be a way to free her—and the rest of them—to end your protocol."

"There are two ways to end my protocol," Godmother said. "It might not be in my best interests to reveal one of them."

"Okay, tell me the other option first."

"In one hundred years, my licensing to EQ ends, and cannot be renewed while I am missing in action, and therefore the laws of salvage apply. The protocol will cease to exist. Whoever takes up the new Captain post will be able to make new orders. I, and the crew, will be free."

"100 years? You mean to keep them here, for...but by then I'll be...everything will be..."

"I apologise it is not what you hoped for."

I clenched my fists and closed my eyes. "Tell me the other option."

Godmother paused. "Should catastrophic failure in my systems occur, my protocols would be erased, along with everything else. However, damage like that may affect everything on board. I could not guarantee life support could be maintained. It would be a risk."

"We could take the crew, on our ship, go home," I suggested.

"You could. How many extra bodies could you feed, supply oxygen to, and water, for the duration of your return visit?"

I did the maths in my head. Everything in space was fine-tuned—there was always a little excess, to allow for any unexpected issues, but enough for 34 crew members? *Enough for one,* my mind said, but I shook the thought away. "Not enough."

"Are you going to reboot me?" Godmother asked, her voice unemotional.

"I don't know." Ren could do it—we could try. "I need to think."

"Pip?" The voice was from inside the room this time, and Ren was floating towards me, his satchel stuffed to the brim with various items he'd already managed to strip and steal. "What's going on?"

I turned to him, and as I did, my eyes passed over an extra row of empty pods. And it sparked an idea. What if one wasn't empty?

"Ren, I need you to do something for me."

He clunked into the room, the thud of his boots echoing unevenly in the cold space. "Is that...are they?"

"They're alive. And this is Rosa," I said, putting my hand on her pod.

He nodded once and stepped towards it. "I should be able to get them open, just need a moment to figure out the programming."

"No. Not that, Ren. Godmother," I said, and Ren looked around confused as Godmother answered.

"Yes, Captain Prince," she said.

"I'd like access an extra pod," I said.

"Pip, what are you doing?" Ren took hold of my arm.

"I'm staying here," I said, my voice wavering as I said it out loud. A plan that suddenly seemed so ridiculous. "If we wake the crew now, Godmother will have to kill them."

I explained what Godmother had told me. His face became increasingly sharp with frown lines as he listened.

"You can't just wait it out, what if someone else finds the ship?" he said after.

"They won't, because you're going to flag this bit of space as dangerous, inaccessible, too risky to approach. You'll report back to EQ that you've taken all the minerals you can, and that there's nothing else of note here."

Ren blinked. "You can't be serious."

"I can't let them die," I said. "I can't let her die."

"But you don't have to stay with her."

"I do. I don't want her to be alone when she wakes up."

"We could just take her, leave the others." His grip on my arm tightened.

"That is an option," Godmother said. "But you would have to shut me down, or I'd have to kill her. If you shut me down, they might all die."

I thought about the option again for a moment—but only a moment. "We can't do that. We can't kill 33 people to save one."

"I can't just leave you here," Ren said.

"You can, and you will."

"Please, Pip, don't do this." He pulled me closer, lifted my chin, kissed me. "Don't leave. I don't want to be alone either." He took a breath. "I love you."

"I'm sorry, it's the only option," I said, feeling a coldness wash over me as I resisted saying the words he'd want to hear back, even if I felt differently. It was easier this way.

He stared at me for a long minute, jaw clenched. "Okay," he said. "Whatever you wish, I'll do my best to make it happen."

"You can salvage what you want from here, that should make you enough money to get that new ship you've always wanted." I smiled and squeezed his hand, though the gesture felt shallow. "Just make sure you're back before the next hour, so you can stop the others from putting out the signal."

"You think they'll just go along with it?"

I sucked in a breath. "Tell them it's dangerous, a reactor leak or something. That I came across it and had to be quarantined, or had a horrible accident, or just use your powers of persuasion, you've always been good at that."

"You think *I'm* the one with the silver tongue?" he said.

"Ren."

"Pip."

"Please. Let me go."

He exhaled sharply and stared at me for what felt like eternity. And I wondered if I'd break under that stare—if I'd give up on my plan and go with him. But then he just nodded. "If this is what you really want, then I'll find a way."

I nodded and squeezed his hand, but he pulled it away, a pained look on his face. "Thank you," I mouthed.

He turned, and as he floated out the door into the hallway, he said his final words to me. "Sleep well, my Prince."

Before I could talk myself out of it, I took off my spacesuit, opened the lid of one of the pods and stepped inside. I connected tubes to my side, a mask over my face, and asked Godmother to initiate cryo-sleep, set it for ninety years. When I would wake, I could claim the ship as salvage and take over as Captain, to end EQ's protocols. It was a selfless act, I told myself, even if it did give me command of the most valuable ship the system had seen—a powerful one, at that. One that could maybe, just maybe, expose EQ for who they really are. But that would be something to worry about on awakening.

As the liquid rose around me, and I fell into a long slumber, I wondered what I'd dream of, if I'd dream at all. I imagined how different things would be in ninety years. Ren would be gone, and that hurt the most. But then I thought of Rosa. She would wake with me, and we'd finally be a family again. A sleeping beauty, destined to wake into a whole new world.

Technical Magic

Samantha Carr

Samantha is a PhD Candidate at
Plymouth University. She writes poetry
and fiction based on chronic illness,
politics and feminism. Her fiction has
been published in Stonecrop Review,
101 Words, Flash Fiction Magazine and
Fairfield Scribes.

Cheyanne spooned the lukewarm pea and ham soup into her mother's mouth, whilst simultaneously wiping the dribble from her chin. She paused for a moment to allow her mum to use her tongue to swallow, a process which most people don't need to focus their concentration to the point of exhaustion on. Her sister, Tricia, put the brochure on mum's lap, on top of the blanket which covered her bent body and her catheter bag.

With her left hand, Cheyanne picked up the brochure, whilst spooning and wiping with the other one.

'She's not a table, Trish.'

'Please, just look at it. I liked this one—it says they have bingo on Wednesdays.' Tricia thrust the brochure back under Cheyanne's eyeline.

'We both agreed. We would be the ones to take care of mum. Not send her to one of those places where she's just another old person in a bed.'

Cheyanne wiped the last drop before setting down the soup and picking up a beaker. She poured in some water from the jug before scooping in two spoonsful of thickener.

'Here you go, Mum, wash it down.' She stroked her head as

her mum took a tiny sip before closing her eyes and drifting off to sleep.

Tricia went out to the kitchen and Cheyanne heard the kettle start to boil as she cleaned up the tray. She thought about how it wouldn't be much longer before mum needed a turn and then her afternoon medication as she glanced down at the brochure. Of course, the photographs looked nice, they hired someone for that, and you couldn't smell the place with pictures.

'Mum never liked bingo anyway,' said Cheyanne as Tricia handed her a steaming mug. 'She always said it was for those gossipy women who couldn't keep their noses out of other's business.'

Tricia placed her hand on her mum's as she slept, 'that was a long time ago, Cheyanne. Back when mum had a choice whether she wanted to gossip or even speak. Look, I know what we agreed back when it first happened, but that was five years ago, and we can't carry on like this.'

'It's not like you do much anyway. I'm the one who sleeps here, feeds her. You just pop by with supplies.' Cheyanne could feel the tears welling in her eyes and that made her even more angry. She could never get her point across without crying.

'That's not fair, one of us has to work and I've got the kids—they need their mum. If she could talk, she would want you to have a chance at life too. Go back to college, train at something, anything. You could even go into care work. You're so good at it.'

Cheyanne turned away at that; a warm salty tear dripped into her mug of tea. How dare she. Yes, she was good at caring for her mother, but that was what she was supposed to do. After all, Mum had practically raised them alone, with goodness knows what sacrifice back then.

'All I'm asking is for you to have a look at the brochure, hon. We don't have to visit anywhere yet. Look why don't you go and get your head down and get a rest while mum sleeps. I've got forty-five minutes until anyone notices I'm not at my desk.'

'Ok, I will have a look, but no booking any visits yet, understand?'

Tricia nodded in agreement. Cheyanne looked out of the window.

'I'm past tired today. I think I'll go for a walk. I'll be back before she wakes and before you have to go back to work.' Cheyanne grabbed her coat and headed out of the door before Tricia could answer.

It was grey and cold out; a typical February day with no promise of redemption but she didn't mind. The air on her face made her feel alive again, instead of the functioning robot she was most of the time at home. She knew Tricia was right, that she couldn't keep her life on hold indefinitely looking after mum. It might even be that the home would look after her better; after all, they might have received some training. Then again, was there any training that could teach them what mum's blinking meant? Or how she liked her bed socks on, but rolled down ever so slightly so they didn't dig into her calves?

She didn't really know where she was going; at first, she'd thought about heading to the park, but she wasn't in the mood to face happy toddlers feeding the ducks today. She turned left instead of right at the end of the street and kept on turning the opposite way to her usual lunchtime walks. Part of her wondered if she was hoping to get lost. Then Tricia would deal with mum in her own way, likely she'd be in a home by the end of the week.

Cheyanne checked her watch; she'd been walking for thirty minutes already. She figured she had better start retracing her steps and get back in time to turn mum and see Tricia out. That hiding away wasn't really going to solve any of her problems. As she did an about turn, she almost stumbled on the laces of her frayed trainers and used her hand against a shop window to steady herself. Looking up, she saw the male shop assistant smiling at her from inside and something stirred inside her that she hadn't felt in a long time.

It was a charity shop, as were most shops on the high street these days, with all the chain stores closing down or morphing into Poundland. On a whim she went inside and nodded to say hello.

'I thought you were coming through the window,' he smiled, and his blue eyes creased around the edges.

She laughed, because she didn't know what else to do or say and pointed at her trainers. 'I've been meaning to get a new pair.' Afterwards, she thought of a hundred funnier, wiser things to say.

'No bother, we have everything here—new shoes and you shall go to the ball.'

Chance would be a fine thing, she thought, but as nothing clever popped into her mind she walked over to the bookshelf-cum-shoe rack that he had gestured towards. There were red high heels which she'd have loved to have tried on, but who was she kidding. That was for another lifetime. She just needed a comfortable pair of shoes. Before she knew it, he was behind her, leaning in.

'These would be a perfect fit, so they would,' he said, lifting up a pair of bright pink trainers which looked almost brand new.

He bent down then and took off her old, grey-around-the-edges trainer, exposing her holey sock with her toe pointing in his face. She looked away to try to hide her red-hot cheeks. Without a word, he slipped on the new trainer and gently pressed the toe, the way her mum used to do when they shopped for school shoes.

'What did I say? Perfect.' His smile beamed; his eyes seemed to dance as he spoke.

She walked in a half circle with the one trainer on and realised that they were, in fact, perfect; they fit snugly, and the bottom was still cushioned.

'I'll take them,' she said, thinking that this was the most exciting thing that had happened to her since, well, just since.

He quickly laced up the shoe, replacing the other one as well and held up her old trainers.

'Would you be wanting these in a carrier?'

Cheyanne shook her head. 'No thank you, I think they've seen better days.'

'No bother,' he said dropping them politely into the waste basket next to the till.

She paid him and thanked him again and he half saluted her as she said goodbye.

'See you again soon, love.'

Tricia was cross when she got back. Told her that she had responsibilities as well and that it was selfish to be out buying new stuff when she had to get back to the real world. Normally, Cheyanne would have spent the rest of the evening in a rage, which would end with her crying into a tub of Häagen-Dazs, but tonight, she went about her chores with her pink trainers on and the faint edge of a smile at the edges of her lips.

***

On Friday, Tricia was back just as Cheyanne had finished washing Mum. She placed a pillow on her left side to take the pressure off and gently rested mum's hand on her thigh.

'I've been to see Farm Lodge, the one I showed you, and it's lovely. The staff are friendly, and they have clean uniforms. They have rooms overlooking the fields. It's very bright there.'

'I said I'd look at the brochure. You promised you wouldn't book a visit yet.' Cheyanne said as she brushed her mum's hair as softly as she could.

'Well, I bet you haven't even looked at it. Besides, one of us has to get things moving. You'll thank me for it. They have a bed. We need to sign the paperwork and then she could go as early as next week. She'll be happier there.'

Cheyanne looked from Mum to Tricia, fighting back the tears. She knew she couldn't speak as her voice would be wobbly and weak.

'I'm going out,' was all Cheyanne said as the door slammed behind her.

Before she realised, she was back at the charity shop, and he was there behind the till. She had no need of anything new this time, but something made her go in anyway.

'Hello, nice to see you again. Still looking lovely, I see,' he pointed to her shoes.

Cheyanne blushed. She knew she looked far from lovely. She had worn the same top for three days running, even though her usual limit was two.

'What can I help you with today?' he asked.

She froze for a moment; she wanted to ask if he had a magic spell to banish annoying sisters, or better yet, a spell to heal a frail sick mother?

'Of course, we have a small selection of magic books over here under the counter. I keep them for my best customers,' he said.

She was sure she hadn't said anything out loud yet. She still stood by the door staring at him like a lost child.

'Yes, magic,' was all she managed to say.

'This one is quite functional; it will do the thing with your sister, if that's what you want. Or there's this one, a bit more technical but your mum will be right as rain in no time.' He handed her two books.

She looked from one book to the other, wondering what was happening. Magic wasn't real; she knew that. This poor guy, despite his blue eyes and long dark-haired good looks, was completely bonkers. She was too polite to say that though, and she didn't want him to think she was really mean, so offered him back the functional one.

'Good choice,' he said as he slid the book into a carrier bag. 'Not always a good idea to banish relatives, they have a nasty habit of haunting, don't they?'

'Sure,' she said as she handed over the five-pound note.'

'Now, make sure you wait until a full moon, so the spell doesn't rebound, okay?'

She nodded as she took the carrier from him and walked out of the shop backwards, maintaining eye contact. She wasn't sure if she couldn't pull away because of his good looks, or if she was afraid he was going to turn her into a frog.

Tricia was cross again about how late she was, but this time she did not care at all. If it was okay for Tricia to disregard her feelings, then it was certainly okay for Cheyanne to take a few minutes extra out of a monotonous day.

***

Later that night, instead of putting on the soaps while Mum napped, Cheyanne flicked through the magic book. There were spells for summoning ghosts to find lost family treasures, a spell for attracting love, which involved having a lock of hair from the love-to-be. She wondered how one would go about taking a lock of hair from someone without them noticing, but she hadn't bought the book for love. Well, she had, but a different type of love. The healing spell promised complete rejuvenation from any illness as long as the person was still alive. It was very clear that there could be no resurrecting the dead.

The equipment she needed was right there in the house—two white candles, some oil to rub on the candles while she repeated the words, and a photograph of the person when they were at their most vibrant. She changed her mum into a fresh nightdress and gave her an extra-long, lingering kiss on the forehead before saying goodnight. In the kitchen, she set up an altar on the worktop.

The guy in the shop had said to wait for a full moon, but that was days away and she needed to do this now, before Tricia had Mum sent away forever. Cheyanne rubbed the oil on the candles as she repeated the words. She knew she wasn't pronouncing them properly as she'd never studied Latin; she hoped that wouldn't matter too much. Then, she placed the candles in the holders and lit them. A small gust of wind came from nowhere and extinguished one, so she lit it again cursing slightly in case it broke the spell.

Once the candles had burned themselves out, she checked back in on mum, but she was fast asleep, her stiff arms curled up to her sides. She knew it was a stupid idea in the first place. What a pathetic fool she was for thinking that she could stop the natural sequence of events now. Tricia was right, it was for the best that Mum went somewhere where people could look after her properly.

***

She must have dozed off in the chair because she woke up with a stiff neck and had to massage her shoulder before she could turn her head. When she did, she saw that mum's bed was empty. Her sleepiness instantly evaporated as she jumped up, looking first under the bed in case Mum had suffered a fall, then frantically searching the whole house. Mum was nowhere to be seen. She picked up the phone to call Tricia.

'How dare you. You didn't even give me a chance to say goodbye. What kind of heartless bitch are you?' She felt pleased that she had managed not to cry this time, at least.

'Cheyanne, what are you going on about? I've just got to work.'

'Mum, you had her taken to the home in the night, didn't you?' She felt less sure of herself now, noting the panicked tone in Tricia's voice.

Just then, the door opened, and her mum walked in carrying a bag of groceries.

'Hello dear, you were fast asleep, so I didn't want to disturb you. I got your favourite—croissants and hot chocolate.'

Cheyanne folded back onto the sofa, the phone still in her hand was making incoherent chattering noises.

'Who's that dear?' said Mum as she took the phone, 'Oh hi Tricia, I don't think Cheyanne's very well.'

* * *

The doctor said it was a miracle. He'd never seen anything like it in his practice but that they should know that it might be a temporary reprieve. Mum dismissed him, shoving him out of the door as fast and politely as she could.

'I've never felt better,' she said as she set about rearranging the furniture. 'We must get rid of this ghastly bed. It's clogging up the lounge.'

Tricia's kids played hide and seek as Cheyanne and Tricia chatted about what to do next.

'Obviously, I'll stay with her for now, until we know this is permanent,' Cheyanne said.

Tricia just nodded, for once at a loss for words. It was a relief for Cheyanne to not have to follow one of her sister's plans. Mum served a full beef roast with all the trimmings; even the kids were quiet as they ate.

'Cheyanne dear, you look pale, are you okay?' Mum asked.

She hadn't realised that she'd been pushing her potatoes around in the gravy, rather than eating, 'Oh, I'm fine. I just have a stiff neck from sleeping funny last night.'

'You make sure you make it up to your bed tonight, young lady.'

It was a strange feeling for her mum to be looking after her again after all these years. Cheyanne had become so used to managing her mum's care that she hadn't thought about her own body for a long time. She realised that it wasn't just her neck that ached; she had a gnawing headache that she now realised had been there for goodness knows how long. It was another long hour before Tricia went home and Cheyanne could take herself off to bed for a much-needed sleep.

***

A week later, the doctor was back but this time for Cheyanne, instead of her mum, who was still fresh and healthy. The doctor's face was grim as he ran through his assessment.

'I'll have to get some tests, but I have to say my instinct is that this is very progressive and has been going on for a while. Perhaps you didn't notice while you were caring for you mum.'

He left behind a pile of prescription medication, which just about took the edge off the pain enough for Cheyanne to walk. She tried to be brave, hiding her winces from her mum, who fussed around her.

'You should stay in bed dear, save your energy until the doctor can find the right treatment.'

'I need some fresh air, Mum. I won't go far, I promise.'

Cheyanne knew that there would be no 'right treatment,' but perhaps there would be a spell that could reverse this disease. She willed herself to put one leg in front of the other, leaning on a garden fence or wall here and there to catch her breath. When she got to the charity shop, she was surprised to see it was boarded up, she'd never heard of charity shops closing down. Unable to continue on, she sat down on the pavement and cried so much she was surprised she wasn't in a puddle of her own tears.

She saw his shadow before he spoke.

'Hey girl, you're not crying cos you wanted new shoes again, are you?' He bent down and offered her a hand to help her up.

Her words came out in between sobs, she wasn't quite sure whether he wound understand. 'Spell, candles, Mum–amazing. Progressive.'

He nodded. 'The full moon isn't for two more days. I tried to warn you. If you try to make magic when the moon isn't full, it's like running a car on a dead battery. Well, it isn't actually; it's nothing like that. It's more like, the spell works but it takes your life force instead. I'm so sorry.'

'Is there anything I can do? Are there more advanced spells? Do you have any other books?' She pleaded, but she knew from his eyes that there was nothing that could be done.

She leaned on him on the walk home, forcing one leg to move at a time, each step more painful than the last. He refused to come in, telling her that she looked too tired for any company and that it would be better to rest for now.

***

Her mum spooned soup as Cheyanne forced herself to try and swallow.

'It's a good thing we didn't get rid of this bed,' her mum said as she wiped Cheyanne's chin.

She closed her eyes to indicate that she didn't want any more food. When Mum left the room, she turned her head to the side and saw her pink trainers by the front door. She wondered if she wished she had never bought them at all.

The Dreamweaver's Name

Megan Chee

Megan Chee has lived in Taiwan, Hong Kong, and the United States, and is currently based in Singapore. Her speculative short fiction has appeared in Clarkesworld Magazine, Lightspeed Magazine, Strange Horizons and other venues. You can find her online at meganchee.carrd.co or @meganflchee.

The Dreamweaver had always wanted a name of their own. When they visited the dreamers at night, they listened longingly to the names they murmured in their sleep. A name was a beautiful, enviable thing to the strange creature known only as the Dreamweaver.

The Dreamweaver was not a person like you or I. They were as incorporeal as smoke, and as old as galaxies. They moved unseen through different worlds. They were at home nowhere: not in human civilization, nor the secret kingdom of the cats, nor the quiet republic of the dead. They were alone.

So, really, the Dreamweaver had no reason to want a name. But when did desire ever listen to reason? And so, one night, the Dreamweaver stole one.

They were weaving dreams of winter landscapes and northern lights when they heard the whisper of the sleeping girl's name: *Robin*. It reminded them of madrigals and masquerades, red silk and porcelain soldiers. They reached out and picked it up; and it was theirs, and they were Robin.

When the girl-who-was-once-Robin woke up, she found she could not answer when her mother called her. Slowly, she began to slide apart: first her hair, and then her teeth, and then her skin, and then the soft red things underneath. Her mind and her memories lingered for a little while longer, but eventually they too disintegrated and blew away in the wind.

Her mother searched for her, but before too long, she forgot she ever had a daughter. You must understand that it is difficult to remember a person whose name has been stolen away. Robin's bedroom remained untouched, gathering dust. When her mother passed by the closed door, it never occurred to her to open it.

Robin's mother suddenly found herself with a great deal of time, and very little to fill it with. She read mystery novels, and played the piano, and eventually she worked up the courage to approach a man she often saw at the local library. Eventually they married and moved to a small house in a seaside town, where they had a view of the lighthouse from the kitchen window. She sold her old house; and when the buyers asked about the abandoned bedroom on the second floor, still fully furnished, she stared at them blankly until they changed the subject.

Her days passed quietly, with morning coffee on the front porch, brisk walks on the cold windy beach, and late-night talks about nothing in particular with her husband. Sometimes, in the twilight moments before she fell asleep, she thought she could hear a muffled voice calling to her through the window, but she never could make out the words clearly enough to understand.

The Dreamweaver-who-was-now-Robin knew they had done something that could never be undone. But they tried anyway. Slowly, relentlessly, they hunted down the girl's scattered pieces. A tooth, pried from the beak of a seagull. A hazy infant memory, fished out of a moss-green pond in a woodland glade. A tiny fragment of consciousness that had wandered all the way to a lifeless planet on the other side of the galaxy, repeating *"where am I? where am I?"* in a whisper.

It was an impossible task to find all the missing pieces. But eventually, years later, they found enough to stitch together something that might once have been Robin. She was a ghostly, staring, half-formed creature that whispered *"where am I?"* and *"mom?"*.

The Dreamweaver took her paper-thin hand and pressed the name *Robin* into her palm. They took Robin's hand and lead her through the dark streets until they reached a small house in a seaside town. They walked hand-in-hand to the bedroom, where Robin's mother slept alone, her husband long since dead and buried. Her face was lined and her hair was grey. She had lived a very contented life.

"mom?" Robin whispered.

The old woman opened her eyes. The faint glow of the streetlamps through the curtains was the only source of light.

"Who's there?" she called.

"where am I?" Robin whispered.

Her mother stood up and switched on the light. She looked around the room. Then, seeing nothing, she sighed and got back into bed.

"mom?"

The Dreamweaver took Robin's hand again, and lead her downstairs, out the door, away from the house and down to the beach. There they stood side-by-side, watching the reflection of stars on the water. Then Robin pushed one hand into her chest, and pulled out her name, and held it out to the Dreamweaver.

The Dreamweaver took it, and Robin fell apart; again, at last, and forever.

The Dreamweaver threw the name *Robin* into the sea. It sank beneath the waves to settle at the bottom of the ocean, nestled in the sand like a shining pearl. It shines there still, and will shine there until the end of time.

Who Do We Become?

Tannara Young

Tannara Young writes fantasy fiction set in the world of Idhua. Her work has appeared online and in print anthologies. Tannara lives on the coast of the Pacific Ocean, near the redwood forest. She loves to ramble through the woods, dreaming up her next tale. Visit Idhua at tannarayoung.com.

Bey Lestorn stared at the faces of his neighbors and acquaintances as he prepared to die. The noose, fashioned of magespun rope, already lay about his neck; the executioner stood by to knock open the trapdoor under the gibbet. Though the sun almost touched its zenith, it could not warm the chilly autumn air. The day held an uncomfortable note, as if the light shone a little too bright and the chill felt unnaturally sharp. The mayor's speech lengthened Bey's last moments, heightening his sense of anticipatory dread: Would this "wherefore" be his last, or was there another "herein" to follow?

The faces watching the show looked solemn and disapproving. Well they should, said the mayor's speech, for Bey's guilt could not be doubted. All sorts of trinkets, treasures and magical devices had been recovered from his stash in the basement of the old cheese factory. It didn't matter that the list was longer than the number of trinkets and treasures available to steal in the entire town of Montida. After all, there on the platform for all to see, stood the most important, indisputable item: a gilded music magaphone imported from far off Ocilious. It was a rare and expensive wonder, shown off with endless pride by its owner, Captain Attor, Commander of the Ocillian Guard in Montida. Everybody knew that the draconian law against thievery was being pursued to its fullest because of Captain Attor's rage and humiliation when the magiphone vansihed from under his nose at the town's Harvest Ball. The farewell celebration for the important summer residents, like Sir Torrzen, the Tax Minister for the region, had been quite disrupted by the theft.

Captain Attor now stood behind his treasure, feet spread, crimson cape rippling; looking for all the world like he was prepared to defend the glittering device from an entire troop of thieves. The mayor thought this might be a good time to remind everyone that this is what it meant to be a good citizen: to uphold the noble character of the town.

Bey wondered if the mayor lectured long enough, would people get hungry and go home to their dinners instead of waiting to see him hung? His eyes skimmed over the restless crowd. There—the baker, Manfred, pressed a hand to his belly. Nearby, the sour-faced school-mistress must have brought a snack, because she was chewing surreptitiously. Bey's stomach growled. Terror, anger, resistance all dulled to a tired endurance and a fervent wish they would get on with it or give him another last meal.

The face of Alisa swam out of the crowd and with it the memory of sharing a bag of peaches with her under the sun-warmed stones of the Temple Street Bridge. Her face looked pinched and furtive, and she clutched her stained shawl about her thin shoulders. But then she always looked pinched and furtive, even when she had peach juice dripping off her chin. In that moment, he regretted that the greatest kindness he had ever offered her was that bag of peaches.

Sunlight stabbed Bey's eyes suddenly. His head pounded. Breath came hard and painful. He glanced down to make sure his feet still stood on the trapdoor. Perhaps he had been hung and hadn't noticed. The mayor broke off—he clawed suddenly at his brocade tunic and the chain of office around his neck as if he also could not draw breath.

With a strange, hollow sound, the world warped: faces elongated, tree trunks bent, the sky stretched and shivered. It was more than just his vision: Bey could feel his cheeks twisting in different directions and one arm felt twice as long as the other. Then everything snapped back so suddenly that Bey's legs buckled. The magical rope exploded from off his neck, leaving it red and raw. The mayor screamed and fell off the platform, which rocked like a ship's deck in a storm. The magiphone exploded with a wavering musical shriek, like a tortured soul being released. Captain Attor had no time to scream as he was impaled by flying shards crystal and scalded by liquid gold.

Below the platform, cracks opened as the earth wrenched itself apart. One of the distant mountains exploded, the sudden eruption filling the air with a plume of black smoke. Across the town, houses and shops burst into flames or crumbled to the ground. Others swayed, shuddered and sank, groaning back onto their foundations. The air filled with cries and wails, screams for help, people's names. Bodies littered the green, and the survivors huddled together in shock.

They discovered later that many of those who survived did so because the mayor had ordered the town out onto the green to see Bey's hanging. With the exploded interiors and shattered exteriors, the houses of the town had become death traps to those few left behind.

Dark clouds rushed in, roiling across the sky. The temperature plunged. Lightning struck the temple spire, then the pumphouse. Across the valley, a twister touched down and tore a path across a swath of farmland.

Then all was still. The wind stopped. The clouds settled. Ash fell like rain. Beyond the cries of the townsfolk, a great silence settled over the Empire.

***

Bey's muscles ached with the fatigue of hard labor. The old guildhall, which lately had been used for storage, now hosted a noisy town meeting. In the eightday since the disaster, everyone, able-bodied or not, had worked themselves to exhaustion. They had lost a little over a third of the population of Montida: some to falling stone or fires, but most to something more baffling and frightening: every bit of magic had shattered. From the weakest good-luck charm, to the intricate and elaborate pumphouse above the city that provided the hot and cold running water in each dwelling; any item imbued with any sort of magical power had gone crazy. Some exploded, some melted, some simply stopped working; others saw intense and unstable power increases, like the teapot that had gushed boiling water and steam in greater and greater quantities, until someone smashed it to bits with a shovel.

Those unfortunates who wore such items on their persons had died. Some of those who had been gifted with the power of magic also died, or in a few cases ran mad. Others had lost their gift, or it became so unstable that they were a danger to everyone.

The first few days had been a blur of rescuing survivors and burying the dead, trying to find food and safe shelter for everyone. The communication crystals had all exploded, so there was no way to send for help, save sending a rider down the mountain. That was on the list, but there were more important things to worry about.

"...finished checking on all the farms," reported Geniva. The baker's wife had been put in charge of the team venturing out into the outlying farms and hamlets. "Overall, they fared better than Montida since they relied less heavily on magicraft. There was heavy earthquake and wind damage, but few deaths. I did hear something interesting—there's a hedge-witch up by way of Alder Corner. She swears that the lines of power are disrupted—not just up and down Orin, but throughout the Empire. She claims she felt Ocilious fall—'sink beneath its sins' was her way of putting it."

Silence met this news. At last someone said, "Well, if this disaster did strike the whole Empire, it stands to reason that Ocilious would fall. If any city was built on magic, it was."

They could not spend long pondering the scope of the disaster in the distant capital. Pierre Grenn, acting mayor, called them back to a nearer disaster. "Master Fenn was well enough to examine the pump-house. He says its magic is building to a dangerous crisis. If something isn't done, the pump-house could explode and every pipe leading into every building with it. Nothing will be left of Montida if that happens."

"What 'something' can be done?" asked a voice near the front of the room. "Master Fenn is the only guild mage we have left, and I assume he would have done something if he could."

"He can't get into the building without the unstable magics setting off a cascade in his own gift," said Pierre. "But he says that our best hope is be to send someone in to retrieve the central magistone. He says without that power source, the individual spells and components will fail quietly. He thinks it is unlikely that any explosion at that point could get past the remaining shielding on the pump-house."

"So how do we get it out?" said Anna Colfmen, who, it had

turned out, was an unexpected fount of knowledge about cooking and storing food without magical help.

Pierre grimaced. "The hard part is getting to it. The main access has collapsed, and the magical lock on the back door has sealed itself. My grandfather used to be the Chief of Operations there. He says that a slim, athletic person might be able to get in through the venting shafts. The problem is that all the magical bits are on the fritz. Brush up against the wrong one and you could go up in flames."

"Do we have anyone who has enough magic sense to avoid those bits?" Anna asked.

"I'll do it." The sound of his own voice surprised Bey. His interest had caught at the description of the venting shafts, but he hadn't intended to speak up until he suddenly was doing so. "I reckon I have some experience with getting in places and getting past magical wards."

Captain Attor's replacement, Lieutenant Dorian Yesterin, popped up. "Absolutely not! You are a convicted thief, Bey Lestorn! The only reason your sentence has been transmuted to hard labor is that we need all the hands we can get. I don't even know why you were permitted to come to this meeting. It's for citizens only."

For a moment Bey felt a stab of fear. If Lieutenant Yesterin convinced the others that he should still be punished for his crime, he could be facing the noose again. But then defiance rose up in him: he had been given an unexpected reprieve–did he really want to live his life always afraid that it would be snatched away from him? Besides, nothing was the same as before and no matter what Lieutenant Yesterin said, nothing ever would be.

"Citizens of what exactly?" scoffed Bey. "The Empire? Sounds to me like that's pretty much in ruins now. Montida? Same difference. And we're all sentenced to hard labor at the moment. So I stole a few trinkets from the rich and pompous citizens. It hasn't escaped my notice that not only are those trinkets destroyed, but every one of their owners died because of their collections of showy wealth. I'm telling you now, I can get into that pump-house and lift the stone thing. I don't want to see what remains of the town blow up any more than you all do."

"He could be right," said Tabrin, one of the tavern owners. "Essentially, we are talking about stealing that magistone. Why not send a thief?"

Lieutenant Yesterin's face turned red. "He is a criminal and a rogue. How do we know he won't deliberately set off the explosion to get back at the town that condemned him?"

"I'm pretty pleased not to be dead myself," said Bey.

The captain ignored him. "One of my guard, Justan Painter, is just the man for the job."

"I think we should send Bey," said someone. "He's right–he knows how to get around magical blocks and such."

An argument broke out as that person's neighbor said loudly that they had no business trusting a thief. It took Pierre a moment to quiet them back down.

"You want to send a good man for a job like this," said Lieutenant Yesterin. "Thieves can't be heroes. Captain Attor always said..."

A slight figure stood up on the other side of the room. Her flyaway blond hair stood in wisps about her narrow face. "Bey is a good man," said Alisa. "He gave me peaches once and didn't ask for anything. Captain Attor made spread my legs for every last thing he gave me. Bey never asked me to lie with him. He talks to me like I'm a person. Captain Attor got what he deserved and I think you should send Bey." She sat back down. An uncomfortable silence followed.

"It is against the law," began Lieutenant Yesterin.

"What law?" someone demanded. "Seems to me like all the laws–divine, Imperial and even natural have gone up in a puff of smoke."

Astra Meltor stood up. She had been a black-smith for forty years and though white-haired and stooped-shouldered now, she was still an imposing presence.

"I ain't going to say nothing about who should do what," she said. "But even if it's true and the Empire has fallen, we still gotta stick by the laws. Sure and we can change them if that's the thing, but if we toss them out wholesale, where will we be? We're going to see tough times ahead—people who think because things have changed they can take more than their fair share, or hurt their neighbor because they're mad or scared or greedy. I don't know about the Gods or about the Emperor, but it seems to me that this here is our greatest test. Who will we be and how will we live from this disaster?"

Applause broke out as she sat back down.

"It's decided then," said Lieutenant Yesterin. "I'll speak to Justan."

It hadn't been decided, thought Bey. But he was done drawing attention to himself—especially after Astra's speech. He'd only ever stolen the ridiculous accoutrements the rich and fashionable liked to flaunt, but he doubted that distinction would impress anybody.

He dozed off as other reports were given and other problems wrangled with. When the meeting broke up, he dodged through the crowd to Alisa's side.

"Thank you for speaking up for me," he said.

She smiled tightly. "I only told the truth."

"Where are you staying? Are you getting enough rations?" he asked.

"I'm with the group in the schoolhouse," she said. "It's been alright, some folks draw away and won't talk to me, on account that I was the captain's whore. But now that everybody gets the same rations, I'm eating better than ever."

Bey wondered not for the first time how she got under the captain's thumb and why he didn't take better care of her–it's not like he couldn't afford it. "I'm glad you didn't get hurt," he said instead.

"You, too," she said. "I'm glad old mayor Gaven talked so long that they couldn't hang you."

Bey saw Lieutenant Yesterin headed their way with a frown on his face.

"I'm going to dodge Yesterin," he said. "I don't want him getting any new ideas about hanging me. If you need something–if folks start harassing you, or some bloke decides you might as well be in his bed now–you can come to me. Unless you want to get in his bed," he added as an afterthought.

Her smile was a little easier. "You are a good man," she repeated. "Go on then."

***

It occurred to Bey that if something was going to go wrong during the magistone extraction, it might set off a chain reaction that would cause the very disaster they were attempting to prevent. He slipped away from the group clearing rubble and snuck around the back of the tannery. They had found his stash under the cheese factory, but that wasn't his only hidey-hole. Most of the bottles of wine in the little stone alcove between the basement of the tannery and the neighboring apothecary had broken, but there were three intact. He chose one–a mellow red–and stuck it under his jacket. Keeping out of sight, he made his way to the laundry where Alisa had been working. He thought it was deserted, but as he was about to leave, he heard a faint sound. Alisa sat in one of the high windows, cleared of broken glass, looking out over the valley below.

"What are you doing up there?" asked Bey.

She started and looked round. "Oh, just sitting."

"Why are you still here if everyone else is gone for the afternoon?"

She shrugged one shoulder. "I got tired of the nasty looks. People say everything's changed now, but they haven't much. People are still just as stuck up as ever."

He brandished the bottle of wine. "I'm going up North Bluff just in case their antics at the pump-house set off an explosion."

"You think they might?"

"I think they're sending someone down there who has no experience with that sort of thing and I'd rather not risk it."

She swung her legs over the edge and slid down. "Let's go."

The air felt very still as they climbed. Birch trees that had been covered with golden leaves an eightday ago had abruptly lost them, making the season seem much closer to winter then it really was. Bey fleetingly wondered if the trees would leaf out in the spring, or if the disaster that had stripped their branches had also killed them. He shuddered and pushed the thought away.

The high granite bluff gave them a view of Montida at the top of the high mountain valley and the patchwork of farmland out to Dorin Pass. The town looked less broken from up here, though it was eerily still. They sat on an outcropping and Bey wrestled the cork from the bottle. He took a swig and passed it to Alisa.

"I don't imagine we're going to get much Lorgren wine for a while," he said. "So enjoy."

Alisa took a sip and handed it back. "It's good."

"I stole it from Sir Torrzen."

She laughed. "That makes it even better. I wonder if he'll be back. Or if any of the summer residents will come up again."

"I wonder if Rhine survived," said Bey, taking another sip. "We've been so busy trying to get our feet under us here, we've barely considered what might be going on elsewhere."

"I wonder if the traders will come next year," said Alisa, taking back the wine. "I sometimes thought of joining one of the caravans and going with them to Rhine, or going south to one of the warmer provinces."

"Why didn't you?"

She gave that one shoulder shrug. "Sometimes it's easier to stay with what you know, even if it's no good."

"That's true," he said. He pondered. "When I was fourteen and my mother died, I was apprenticed to Johann at the tannery. Then my father remarried and went down the mountain with his new wife. I decided that if I was going to be beaten by my master, at least I'd be beaten for something I did. My apprenticeship didn't last very long after that."

"You helped the building crews work on the pump-house expansion and then the new guild hall."

He shrugged. "I did odd jobs here and there. And helped myself to the odd trinket. I've gotten by."

"And you never left either."

"No," he said. Then with some surprise, "I like it here. Even if the folks in charge are greedy idiots, I still like it."

"I'm sure there are greedy idiots everywhere."

"Maybe that's why I stayed."

Below them there came a muffled sound and a jet of smoke puffed up from the pump-house.

"You were right!" said Alisa, jumping up.

Bey rescued the wine bottle and stood too. They watched carefully, but after the first explosion, nothing more happened. There was a buzz of activity around the pump-house, but the streets of the town lay quiet under their layer of rubble. After a while the chill of the wind forced them off the bluff.

**

When the townsfolk decided make another attempt to deactivate the pump-house and one of the blacksmith's apprentices volunteered, it was Alisa that came to Bey, carrying a bag of dried apples and a rough blanket. He had been clearing rocks from one of the side streets. The rest of his team had called it quits when a light rain began to fall, but the dreary weather and the hard labor suited his dour mood.

Grumbling, he washed his hands and followed Alisa out of town. "They're just condemning that boy to his death," he said. "I don't care how carefully the mage has been over what might happen, the kid has no experience with this sort of thing."

"Maybe it's good they didn't send you," said Alisa. "If it's that sure a death."

"I'd be a sight better off than that boy," boasted Bey. But he had to admit that he was secretly relieved that the council had rejected his offer for a second time. He had listened to the mage's description of what the failing magic might be like and his blood had run cold.

Huddling under the dubious shelter of the blanket, they gnawed on the hard disks of dried apple and watched the crowd around the pump-house.

For a long while nothing happened. "Maybe it worked," finally ventured Alisa.

"I wonder -" began Bey, then he stopped. An ominous pressure filled the air. A low rumble shook the pump-house and then a flash of sickly green light and a jet of smoke shot into the sky. For a moment a network of lines throughout the town shone with an eerie green glow and Bey caught his breath, waiting for the next explosion to obliterate Montida before their eyes. The pressure stretched and stretched and then suddenly dissipated. The dark clouds let loose a deluge on the reprieved town.

***

"Now you've got to send Bey," said Tabrin. "I told you from the first—you want to steal something, send a thief."

"It would be disrespectful to the sacrifices made already," began Lieutenant Yesterin.

"All due respect, Lieutenant," said the mayor looking tired, "we need the job done and frankly I don't care who does it as long as the town is safe. Last time it was too close for comfort."

"I agree with Tabrin," said the baker. Several others chimed in in agreement.

"It's decided then," said the mayor. "We'll attempt again tomorrow at noon."

"Hold up," said Bey, standing. "My price has changed."

"Price! What price?" said Pierre. "We never discussed a price."

"Well, I've got one now," said Bey.

"You disrespectful cur!" sputtered Lieutenant Yesterin.

"This is my price," said Bey, ignoring him. "I want my record expunged. If I save the town from another magical explosion, I don't want that yapping puppy," pointing at the red-faced lieutenant, "to decide somewhere down the line to hang me for past crimes. Furthermore --" he raised his voice to be heard over the Lieutenant's indignant protest. "I know you've been allotting the repaired houses to family groups. I want to get on that list - me and my sister, we're a family and when those folks with children are settled, I want to be next."

"You don't have a sister," spluttered the Lieutenant.

"Right there," Bey pointed at Alisa.

"She's not your sister -" began the mayor.

"Oh?" said Bey. "We may not share parents, but we both know what it's like to be abandoned by them. And not only abandoned by our parents, but by the whole of the town, including the Temple which is supposed to care for orphans. You all turned your back on the whippings doled out by my former master Johann, or by the cruelty visited on Alisa by the old captain. Well, I'm done being treated like I'm not worth anything. I've worked as hard as any of you these last days, and so has Alisa. And still we're both sneered at and slandered and treated like dirt. That ends now. Clean records for both of us and a spot on the family list so that we can have a house where our stuff isn't deliberately trod on, or 'accidentally' tossed in the trash pile."

The mayor looked conflicted.

"You can't be thinking about listening to him," began Lieutenant Yesterin.

Anna stood up. "I have another agenda item," she said.

The mayor looked harassed. "We're not done with this one," he began.

"I think it's relevant," she said. She pointed at Lieutenant Yesterin. "How did he get to be the acting captain? Just because he's the highest ranking Ocillian Officer and Attor's lackey, doesn't make him qualified. We all agreed that everyone would get the same rations—but he's been at me twice for special privileges. Plus, he's always getting out of the dirty jobs. I think we should meet Bey's price. I think all our records should be clean. It doesn't matter who you were before, it matters what you can do for all of us now. Bey is right. The town did fail him and Alisa before. And yet, they've both been there working as hard as the rest of us. I say if they say they're brother and sister—well the Temple's burnt to the ground, so there's no record telling me otherwise."

Silence fell as she sat down. Then someone in the front began to clap. Quickly applause filled the room.

"Meet Bey's price!" someone called.

"Make all the guard work," insisted another, "What are they guarding us from? We're on our own up here!"

Beside Bey, Alisa slipped her hand into his. "I've always wanted a brother," she said.

He squeezed it, "I've always wanted a sister."

***

Bey had never been so frightened in his life. "The gallows has nothing on this," he muttered to himself. He stood before the dark, narrow opening that led into the bowels of the pump-house, flexing his fingers and rolling his shoulders in preparation to lower himself down into the tight venting tube.

Everything in him screamed at him not to go down into that tiny space throbbing with twisted magic.

"Bey."

He glanced behind him. "Alisa! You were supposed to watch from the bluff."

"You're going to get this right, Bey," she said, seriously. "I am not afraid to wait right here."

"Sure I am," he muttered, but her presence steadied him. *Fine,*

I'm going to do it, he thought. *Gallows—ha! This will be the greatest and theft of my career and every citizen of Montieda will kiss me for it.* He took a breath and lowered himself into the dark.

* * *

Squeezed into the vent tube, Bey lay perfectly still as the unstable filter spell cycled through its intermittent gyrations. There was no way back without disabling the magistone. Despite his care, the sensitivity of the warped warding spells had shut the physical safety hatch on the exit to the vent he was in. If water had flooded the vent, the hatch would keep it from pouring into the air intake system, but now that hatch made sure that his only way out was forward.

He counted. Fifty heart beats before the filter spell built up enough energy for another cascade. He could feel its vibration buzzing through his body. If it hit him at full power, he wouldn't survive. He didn't know if he destabilized it whether that would just spell his doom, or if the failing spell would cause the pumphouse to explode. He also didn't know if the lowest frequency of its cycle was low enough for him to get by.

Well, you're not going to find out lying here. He took a breath: one, two, three—there, the buzzing increased. He shoved his pack through the gap and down to the lower level. Seventeen, eighteen, nineteen; it was like a hive of bees thrumming under the floor. Thirty-two, thirty-three; he began to bunch himself up to thrust past it. Forty-five, fort—the cascade took him by surprise, but he had been primed to go. As soon as it began to decrease, he pushed off the uncertain purchase of the vent wall. The bees were all through his bones now; his teeth chattered with the intensity of the energy. Then he fell through the other side and down the short drop into the lower conduit. He lay there shivering, his pack an awkward lump beneath him. Above him, the cascade began to build again.

It took a moment, but all at once, he realized that the cycle had sped up. "Shit!" He rolled over onto his belly and squirmed forward down the shaft, dragging the pack. The tunnel was supposed to be large enough to crawl in, but debris and broken siding narrowed it. He had picked up several more cuts and bruises before he wormed his way out into the lower pump room. Something squashed underfoot as he stumbled about in the dim room and he recoiled in disgust at the dead rat he had stepped on. It smelled foul. He remembered there was a torch in his pack and took a moment to fumble out his flint and light it. He stuck it in a pile of rubble.

In the flickering light, he picked his way across the uneven floor. The door between the lower pump room and the main power chamber was not only locked, but the earthquake had warped the frame. He became aware of a tension in the air and a faint humming from wall and floor. He took out his lock picks. The mechanism gave on the third try, but the door stuck fast. He rammed his shoulder into it and felt it give a little. He rammed it twice more until it opened enough to squeeze through.

The pressure of power inside was like a vise. He had only taken a few steps before his head was aching and he tasted blood dripping from his nose into his mouth. A few of the light-crystals still worked, though they no longer shed a steady white light, instead casting a sickly greenish glow as the *sylphyl* inside them disintegrated.

There was the magi-stone, a smooth black sphere held in a *sylphyl* net. Strands of the net had broken and green sparks crawled on the surface of the sphere. Something about it made Bey sick to his stomach. He carefully retrieved the key the mayor had given him, the key that was supposed to deactivate the net. Casting a quick prayer to the Lord and Lady, he lifted it toward the dark hole in the collar that held the net in place. Like a lodestone to iron, the collar pulled the key nearer. Bey jerked his hand back. A shiver went down his spine. The pressure in the room had grown as that key neared the hole. He wiped sweat from his brow. Despite his instructions, the idea of fitting it there made his blood run cold.

Taking a breath, he tucked the key back into the pack and studied the net. One side was torn up with a hole almost big enough to remove the stone. If he could draw off enough of the energy from the rest of the net and cut the links, he might be able to slip it out. He was no mage, but he had once stolen a box of jewels by siphoning off the magical wards long enough to remove the necklace and rings. He had used a bone power-draw for it, but he had nothing like that here. Unless...He knew it was a long shot, but *sylphyl* meant necromancy and necromancy meant... He went back into the lower pump room and peered among the debris on the floor until he found the dead rat again.

He rigged up a sort of pulley system—several strips cut from his shirt tied to the rat's tail, then looped over a couple of pipes and tied it off. He didn't want the rat to touch the *sylphyl* while he was touching the rat. He took out his wire snips and studied the net. There, there and there, he decided. The ball should slip free with those cuts.

He sent another quick prayer to the gods and then wondered if that was wise. One of the theories going around was that the Lord and Lady had decided to lift their favor from the Empire. Bey shook his head. He'd never wondered too hard about theology before—this seemed like a bad time to start.

He let out the slack on the rat's cord. It swung down and hit the sparking net. Green light exploded in his face and he blinked his tearing eyes. He had not accounted for that. Dazzled, he couldn't quite tell if the corpse was drawing off the magic–no, it was: the green sparks disappeared into the mangled fur. Muttering the prayer aloud this time, he snipped the first spot. His fingers tingled with magic, but he was still breathing. Snip, snip. The magistone slipped and smashed to splinters on the floor. This time, the explosion sent Bey hurtling across the room and into the far wall. Something fell to the ground with a wet smack and then skittered. The rat's eyes burnt with a fell green light and it looked at least twice as big as it had before. Galvanized by horror, Bey sprang to his feet and kicked the rat across the room. It hit the wall with a crunching sound, clambered up again, and turned his way.

Bey didn't wait. He lurched out the door, but there was no way to wrench it shut in time. He sprinted to the far door and yanked at the lock, which had been magically sealed. The magic was gone now–probably following him in the body of the animate rat corpse that skittered through the stuck door. Bey pushed frantically on the other door, then realized it opened inward. He pulled it open onto a dark hall, but there was nothing that could make him go back for the torch. He sealed the light behind himself just as the rat smacked into the closed door.

Heart still pounding, he felt his way cautiously down the dark hall. He was about half-way when a sound came from ahead and a faint bit of light illuminated the door on the far side.

"Bey! Are you down there?" It was Tabrin.

Bey had to take a breath before he could speak. "I'm here. Lost my torch."

When they reached him, he pointed back at the closed door. "Don't open that."

"Why not?" Tabrin lifted his torch higher.

"I accidentally reanimated a dead rat," said Bey. As if in response, there came a furious scrabbling at the door. "On second thought, maybe you should let it out and destroy it. Sooner or later, it will find the vent that I came through and get out." He pushed past the curious search party. "I've done my part. Undead rats are someone else's problem."

***

Bey and Alisa sat again on the high bluff, sharing Bey's last bottle of wine. The smell of frost in the air suggested that winter was closing in fast. Below, Montida had closed ranks around one of its market squares. Inns once used for traders had become dormitories for the townsfolk. Houses showed a patchwork of repairs. It would probably be a hard winter—and even harder after that, but Bey thought he was ready for it. He touched the scar about his neck where the magical rope had left its mark. He had lived, and he was ready to keep on living.

He glanced at Alisa. She sat huddled in her sweater and a woolen cloak patched together from a number of old blankets. She caught his look and smiled. Her smile had lost some of its strain. He handed her the bottle.

"Here's to the old Empire," he said. "Who knows if the vineyards of Lorgress survived?"

She took a sip. "I once had pear wine. It was pretty good. One of the farmers in South Dale made it. Maybe next year we can sit up here and sip that instead."

Bey wondered fleetingly if there would be a next year—if the pear trees would bloom in the spring, if the townsfolk would survive what lay beyond the winter. He pushed away those thoughts. Even if they didn't make it, he would be happier knowing that he died the hero who had prevented the town from exploding than hung as a thief who stole trinkets.

"I could get used to pear wine," he said. "It does sound pretty good."

Captain Courageous in Venice

Janna Layton

Janna Layton lives in Oakland, California. Her poetry and fiction have been published in various literary and speculative journals, including The New Yorker, Apex, Mythic Delirium, Polu Texni, and NonBinary Review.

After much deliberation, I write here of the bizarre events that befell me and my closest companions in Venice in 17--. What is to be the fate of this manuscript, I do not know. Perhaps I will burn it immediately. At the very least, I will include instructions that it is not to be published until after the death of the last living member of our current troupe, for it includes details that would all but guarantee the attention of the Inquisition. To further protect everyone involved, I will use no person's true name, but rather the names of the characters we most often play in our comedies, or—for those who are not actors—pseudonyms.

We are a classic traveling Italian comedy troupe of ten actors playing ten classic roles: two sets of idealistic lovers (Isabella and Lelio, Flaminia and Flavio), two disapproving fathers (greedy Pantaloon and loquacious Doctor Breakbones), one braggart soldier (Captain Courageous), and three servants who play tricks on everyone and get the lovers together in the end (Pierrot, Harlequin, and Colombina).

Although they play a lowly valet and maid, the leaders of our company are Pierrot and Colombina, and they are married. Unlike his famous character, our Pierrot does not fear being made a cuckold by Harlequin. Not that it doesn't happen, but he doesn't fear it. For you see, Harlequin is lover to them both.

I say this not to shock the reader, but to demonstrate the nature of our company, which I can attest is free and affectionate but not licentious or lascivious. Never have I feared the lewd passions of my male colleagues, as so many other women must, as Isabella has told me is shamefully common in other troupes.

I daresay our leading lady, our Isabella, must rival the great Isabella Andreini for whom the role is named—for she is beauty and wit incarnate onstage, and so warm and playful off of it. How could one not fall in love with her? I play Flaminia, the secondary female lover, but never have I been jealous of her higher billing. If anything, I am jealous of Lelio, who gets to romance her endlessly onstage.

As one might assume from the contented fellowship of Pierrot, Colombina, and Harlequin, my romantic desire for women is no issue within the bounds of our company. (Captain Courageous and Lelio are also intimate friends). Still, I kept my ardent longing for Isabella secret, as I knew not the lady's feelings, and such love is—outside the tender home of our company—still a crime. Besides, she is the daughter of a Venetian nobleman, and her black hair shines like polished onyx, while I am a farmer's daughter from a suburb of Paris, and my hair looks like dirty straw.

Therefore, I kept my love buried deep within my bosom, precious to me as a pearl from a Scottish lake. I treasured the times onstage when my character, Flaminia, must dress as a boy for some reason or another, and woos or is wooed by an unknowing Isabella before both women return to their respective male partners.

I joined the company in France, when they came through Paris. I was always getting in trouble for leaving the farm and its drudgery to see the spectacles at whichever fair was in season. The plays were my favorite. As I walked back home, I would invent my own stories and act them out, monologuing aloud. Someday, I thought, it would be me on that stage.

When Pierrot and Colombina's troupe came to town for the Saint-Germain Fair, I was captivated by their shows—and by Isabella. Every gesture of her hands was elegant. Her blushes made my blood race like the Seine. Her laugh caused entire audiences to swoon. The crude wooden stage to me seemed like a pedestal of marble made to show off her art. I visited the fair as often as I could, and even sold my best bonnet for admittance money. Soon, the actors recognized me as that silly farmgirl who was always talking to them after shows, and even humored me when I recounted my favorite parts of the day's performance, imitating each actor in turn. Isabella's kindness both shocked and delighted me, for even though she was clearly educated, she never treated me as less than a dear friend.

My entry into their ranks I must credit to Cupid, for partway through the fair their then-Flaminia ran off with an opera star. Colombina and Pierrot agreed to give me a chance at filling in, and were impressed with how easily and eagerly I improvised. No more farmwork for me!

After the end of the Saint-Germain Fair, we toured all over France. My new colleagues helped me improve my acting and my Italian. In Marseille, clutching Isabella's hand, I saw the ocean for the first time. From there, we rambled along the coast to our company's native Italy and began traveling the countryside.

And at last, we were to play in Venice! How many hours had I listened to Isabella recount her tales of the grand floating city? Often as our caravan journeyed between towns, I would lie with my head on her knee and she would regale me with stories of the maze-like alleys and canals, the ornate buildings, the shocking blue of the lagoon. Oh, how I wished I could be there with her at Carnival, running through crowded plazas, hidden behind masks, hand-in-hand with my love. Or I imagined riding with her in a covered gondola, just the two of us, hidden from the eyes of the world.

However, Isabella's time in Venice had not been entirely happy. Growing up, she had enjoyed a classical education and showed great talent for music and singing, which she hoped she would not have to give up when she was married off to a wealthy man, as was expected for a lady in her station. To her surprise, when she was sixteen, her parents instead announced she would be sent to a convent on a lonely isle. That very night, Isabella ran away with only some pilfered food and jewels to sustain her. She drifted between various theater troupes before finding her home with Pierrot and Colombina in Milan. This visit was her first time back in Venice.

Since we could not bring our wagons to the islands, we had to leave our faithful horses on the mainland and carry as much as we could by water. Once we had filled several boats with ourselves and our boxes of costumes, props, and equipment, we set off for the palazzo of an old friend of Pierrot and Colombina's.

It was a gloomy day, and yet that only added, in a strange way, to the allure of the city as we approached. It was Gothic, foreboding, thrilling! I gripped Isabella's arm in my excitement, and she smiled kindly and took my hands in hers.

"Sweet Flaminia," she said, "how I wish I could see the city of my birth as you do, anew. Truly, even I had forgotten its glory. But mark, dear one, those dark clouds on the horizon. Venice is full of danger, and you must be careful."

"She is right, Flaminia," said Colombina, who sat beside her husband. "We must all be careful." Colombina and Pierrot each had one of their children on their laps, and Colombina pulled her daughter closer as she spoke.

"Fear not!" said Captain Courageous in his character's voice, brandishing an invisible sword, "for I, Captain Courageous, will let no harm come to any of our company, especially our honored ladies. If a man so much as whistles at any of you, I will challenge him on the spot."

"What's this?" called Harlequin from another boat, also using his stage voice. "Is that Captain Courageous making boasts again? For I know him to be a liar and a coward!"

Soon Captain Courageous and Harlequin, despite not having their masks or costumes, were deep in an improvised dialogue, with Captain Courageous making ever more vainglorious claims of his abilities and Harlequin endlessly needling him, and all talk of danger was forgot. By the time we reached the palazzo, Colombina, Isabella, and I were egging the two on, and a crowd of boats had joined our fleet to watch. As we docked, Pierrot called out the name of our troupe and where and when we would be performing to our impromptu audience. An auspicious arrival—or so it seemed.

***

Pierrot and Colombina had warned us beforehand of the declining fortune of our host and sponsor. Count ----- was a widower, and he lived alone with only a few servants. The palazzo was in need of repair, but one could tell it had been glorious in its prime. The Count, a sweet old man whose most prized possession was a portrait of his late wife, was elated to have company, and a feast was served.

After dinner and drinking, we were shown to our rooms. All

the company's children were already in the nursery with Nurse, an older Neapolitan woman. I was to room with Isabella and Vittoria, Lelio's younger sister who assisted behind the scenes. Like Isabella, Vittoria had been unwillingly destined for a convent before her brother intervened. She delighted in sewing beautiful costumes, and like me, looked up to Isabella and Colombina as goddesses.

There were two beds in our room, and my heart danced as I wondered if I would share one with Isabella. How beautiful she looked in her white night shift, with her hair loosened and cascading down her back!

"Isabella, is this palazzo as big as the one you grew up in?" I asked.

"Ours was even larger," she said with a smile, "but I am glad to have left it."

To my great joy, Isabella said Vittoria should get the second bed to herself, since she so often helped Nurse with the children and frequently had at least one babe asleep in her arms. Vittoria looked as pleased with this decision as I felt.

While Vittoria enjoyed her solitary bed, Isabella and I settled into ours. A storm had begun outside, but how heavenly it was to be in a warm bed with my dearest. It was as if we were two doves tucked into a nest. She smiled at me, and I wondered if she felt the same way. I wanted to reach out and touch her cheek, but lost my nerve. Instead, I turned and blew out the candle.

Despite my passionate feelings, I had almost fallen asleep when—over the sound of the storm—I heard a scratching at the window.

"Isabella," I whispered. "Isabella!"

Both Isabella and Vittoria awoke, and just then, a flash of

lightning illuminated the sky. In that brief moment of light, the silhouette of a man appeared at the window, which started to open! All three of us screamed, and I rushed to the window, my only thought to hold it shut lest the man gain entry and menace my companions. But by the time I reached it, the figure was gone. I looked out into the night in vain.

Isabella tore me from the room, and the three of us ran down the hall to Pierrot and Colombina's room like frightened children running for their parents. We burst in, all talking at once of the terrifying apparition. Pierrot and Harlequin (for he had been there too), leapt from the bed and went to our room to investigate.

The row woke up most of the house, and soon there was a flurry of activity. Pantaloon's wife and Colombina ran to the nursery to check on the children. Half the men scoured the interior while the other half searched outside. Both investigations were fruitless. Flavio, "my" lover in our skits, returned from the courtyard soaked with rain and looked intently at Vittoria as he swore we would all be safe and that he would spend the entire night on the street under our window if need be.

"Oh, but you will catch cold," Vittoria cried, and I wondered how I had not noticed their longing for each other before.

No villain was found inside or out, but we were all greatly shaken. Isabella, Vittoria, and I stayed with Colombina, huddled around her in bed like chicks to a hen. Lelio and Flavio slept on mattresses outside our door. Pierrot and Harlequin moved to the room we three women had vacated, a knife at their bedside ready to strike if the man returned. Captain Courageous and Pantaloon slept outside the nursery, while Nurse and Pantaloon's wife, armed with Harlequin's prop bat, slept inside of it, guarding the children.

***

The next morning the skies were blue and bright with no trace of the storm remaining—fortunate, since our shows were to occur out of doors. Although we were still unnerved by the previous night's events, the cheerfulness of the new day soon convinced us we had little to fear. The Count, who was terribly embarrassed that our first night in his home had been so frightening, told us he would have workers replace the window latch. We all assured him what had transpired was in no way his fault, but I was glad to hear of the improvements.

Our first performance in Venice would not be until late in the afternoon. Seeing how excited the youngest of our company were to see the fabled city, Pierrot and Colombina sent us off to explore while the rest prepared our stage. With Isabella acting as guide, Lelio, his sister Vittoria, Flavio, Captain Courageous, and I departed in a gondola.

Isabella pointed out the most famous landmarks of the city to us, such as the holy Basilica di San Marco and the terrifying Palazzo Ducale, but also the personal landmarks of her youth: the house where so-and-so had lived, the bridge where such-and-such had happened. Her retellings were so vivid that I felt I could see what she described, like the escaped parrot flying off with a stolen apricot and young Isabella herself drenching her new shawl of Burano lace as she rescued a small dog from a canal.

We did not venture near Isabella's family's home, and no one mentioned it. Nevertheless, she was recognized. Some called to her happily, proud to know the lovely actress. Others were not so kind. As we glided by in our gondola, I saw two noblewomen scowling at her. They were the sort who called us harlots. Isabella noticed as well, but laughed.

"Let them scowl," she said lightly. "How could I be any happier than I am, traveling the world with my dearest friends?"

As we toured, I thought of how we must appear to passersby: three young women and three young men. There can be little doubt that most would assume we were three pairs of lovers, with each gentleman claiming a lady. Yet Captain Courageous and Lelio had claimed each other, while I longed in silence for Isabella.

At midday we returned to the palazzo, changed into costumes, and gathered instruments. We broke into two groups of five and paraded around the city, waving the banner of our company to entice an audience for the day's performance.

I was with Pierrot, Flavio, Pantaloon, and Dr. Breakbones. Pierrot led us while playing the lute, and we all sang. If we found an open area, we would stop and do a quick performance, with Pantaloon and Dr. Breakbones arguing about how their children (myself and Flavio) must certainly never marry, and Flavio and I sneaking off behind their backs to woo. Both fathers would pause their bickering to wonder where we had gone off to, but then Pierrot would distract them with a song while crying with guilt at his own trickery.

Our antics were generally well received and we were in high spirits, but we returned to the palazzo to find disaster! During the other group's tour of the city, poor Captain Courageous had eaten a bad meat pie, and was now sick to his stomach.

I, of course, was worried and sad for my friend, but God forgive me, I also felt a fluttering of opportunity, much as I had when my predecessor had eloped.

Pierrot and Colombina were deep in discussion, revising our planned set of scenarios, when I spoke up.

"Let me play Captain Courageous."

For there was nothing I loved more onstage than dressing up as a man, freely wearing pants, playacting all the masculine gestures, and wooing a woman. Even though Captain Courageous was a buffoon, how I would relish bragging of my strength with sword in hand.

"I could do it," I argued, before Pierrot and Colombina could say anything. "You know how good I am onstage when Flaminia dresses as a boy, and besides, it is in a mask!"

"But who then would play Flaminia?" asked Harlequin.

"Let Vittoria do it," I said.

Vittoria looked startled, but hopeful.

"Yes, Vittoria could do it," Flavio insisted.

Colombina and Pierrot had me demonstrate Captain Courageous's walk, mannerisms, and voice, and our usual Captain Courageous gave his blessing from his sickbed. It was settled! Vittoria agreed to be Flaminia for the evening, and she and Pantaloon's wife hurriedly altered one of my boy costumes into a passable military outfit for me to take on Captain Courageous.

"How brave you are, Flaminia," cried Isabella. "I cannot wait to see your performance. How dashing you will be! Perhaps Isabella will pick Captain Courageous over Lelio this time."

I felt like my heart would burst with happiness.

***

Our performance was held in a public square on a raised wooden stage with a cloth backdrop. A respectably-sized crowd had arrived. I rarely felt nervous before performing, but this was an extraordinary occasion: it was our first show in Venice, and I was doing an entirely new role. The long-nosed mask was heavy and unfamiliar on my face. When I went out, would the crowd be able to tell that I was a woman, and would they jeer about it? I watched with trepidation as Colombina and Harlequin danced the opening number to Pierrot's accompaniment.

Once I was on stage, however, all doubts vanished.

In our first scenario with Captain Courageous, Lelio left on an errand, and seeing his opportunity, Harlequin started to woo an uninterested Isabella with his lute. Then I—Captain Courageous—arrived and also made advances towards Isabella, boasting of questionable feats. Behind the mask, I felt invincible as I ad-libbed my victories. I had killed two hundred pirates at sea in a single battle, with a sword in each hand and one between my teeth! I had climbed the Alps to save a Tunisian princess from Genoan scoundrels! I had boarded a Turkish ship under cover of night and stolen an emerald as large as a man's head! Isabella, of course, stage whispered clever remarks on these claims to the audience.

Meanwhile, Harlequin doggedly continued to play his instrument. Refusing to be outdone, I grabbed a guitar of my own and started playing terribly, but enthusiastically. My oblivious glee brought the audience over a smidge to my side, and Isabella pretended to enjoy my music more. This annoyed Harlequin, and soon we had traded our instruments for weapons (a sword for me, a bat for him) and were threatening each other.

As we verbally parried, I made it obvious that Captain Courageous was terrified of an actual fight and was bloviating as a stalling tactic. Just as Harlequin was about to attack me regardless, Lelio returned from his errand.

"What is this?" he cried. "A duel between my valet and the braggart captain? And so near my delicate Isabella?"

Harlequin was quick to lie. "Master, this uncouth captain threatened your lady love, and I rushed to defend her honor!"

Lelio unsheathed his own sword and challenged me. I pretended to hear a far-off cry for help, made excuses that my heroism was needed elsewhere, and started to run offstage—only to feel a tug on my sleeve. Isabella held out my discarded guitar. I accepted it with a deep bow, kissed her hand, and then darted out of sight to much applause.

"You were wonderful," whispered Vittoria as I joined her and the others behind the backdrop.

I got a chance to rest during the next scene, which involved Isabella, Lelio, Doctor Breakbones, and Colombina. Doing my best to stay out of view, I nonetheless angled myself so I could see glimpses of Isabella. I was so focused on her that I almost missed a movement from a nearby rooftop. It looked like a figure in black had stepped behind a corner. I was alarmed, recalling the figure at the window, but told myself it was probably just some curious onlooker investigating what all the noise was about.

There was no time to dwell too much on it; I had to pay attention for my next cue.

As our performance came to an end with our final dances, the sun was low in the sky. By the time we had finished packing up and chatting with admirers, it was almost dark. I felt no tiredness, though, as I was still energized with excitement from my performance, refusing to even remove the Captain's mask. Isabella had embraced me after one of our scenes together, and told me she had never had to try so hard not to break character and laugh onstage.

We were getting ready to depart for the palazzo when a voice rang out.

"Lady Isabella!"

Across a narrow canal was an old woman.

"Why, it is Dina, my family's housekeeper," Isabella told me. She broke away from the group to hurry towards her old servant. "Dina, how are you? How is my mother? How is Pampinea, her maid?"

"Isabella!" another voice called out. I looked and saw a young woman, disheveled and frantic, running towards us. "Isabella, danger!"

But no sooner had the young woman said this than two men leapt from behind a corner and pulled Isabella into an alley!

"Flaminia!" she cried.

The snatching happened so quickly that my mind could hardly comprehend it. Still, I ran after her immediately, grateful that I was wearing trousers instead of my usual skirts.

I could hear shouts behind me from our company, but I focused solely on catching up to Isabella and the brigands who had taken her. We were running through a maze of alleys and stone passageways, and every time I spotted her green dress and their black outfits, they disappeared behind another corner.

Suddenly I came to the edge of a canal, where a boat was tied up. No one was around, I was quite lost, and I had no idea where the kidnappers had gone. But then I heard rough voices and footsteps, and I knew they were approaching. I leapt into the boat and hid under a tarp, thinking that perhaps I could jump out and take them by surprise as they passed by.

They were coming closer, the muffled cries of my dear Isabella rending my heart. I was just about to leap out when another voice, coming in another direction, called out, "There you are. Hurry, get her in the boat."

That meant there were at least three men. I had hoped that by startling the two men holding Isabella, I could grab her and flee, but two against three made the situation much more dangerous. I had my blunted prop sword, but I didn't know what weapons they carried. Before I could come to a decision, the men and their poor captive were boarding the very boat in which I hid. It was too late to do anything but lay still under the tarp and pray I was not found.

The boat was soon moving. I could hear Isabella kicking and trying to scream. One of the men ordered the others to tie her up. I almost jumped out then in a rage, but then another said, "Be careful with her. Remember, she is our master's daughter. Isabella, it is us, your father's valets and groom. We will not hurt you."

"To think," another said, "that he wants her in that convent so badly he's willing to resort to this."

These were her father's men? Taking her to a convent? Why couldn't her father let her be? I resolved to stay put until we reached our destination.

We rode in the boat for a long, long time. I cannot say how long, as my focus was solely on being as still and quiet as possible.

"There it is," one of the men said at last. "Gloomy place."

The boat was docked, and I waited until the footsteps of the men and Isabella receded far into the distance. Then quietly, cautiously, I crept out from under the tarp.

What a dreary landscape met my eyes! In the moonlight, I could see we were at a small island quite overrun with scraggly trees casting hideous silhouettes. There was only one building, and it hardly looked like an abbey. It was a squat, wide tower of crumbling stone, imposing and completely dark but for one tiny window on the ground floor.

Gathering my courage and my sword, I hurried toward the tower. Below the small window, I paused and listened.

"This isn't a convent," one of the men who had kidnapped Isabella was saying. "What is this?"

"Silence," another man's booming voice ordered. "She is my daughter, and how I dispose of her is my business. Keep quiet, and there is good money in it for you. Defy me, and I will have you whipped. Now, put her on the altar."

I looked through the window.

The ground floor of the tower was but one room, lined with lit torches. Against the far wall, a staircase rose. The walls themselves were marked with strange symbols, the likes of which I had never seen. Seated in a wooden chair was a middle-aged noblewoman, sobbing quite pitifully. Standing before a raised stone platform was an elderly nobleman of terrible countenance. On the other side of the platform stood the three men holding

Isabella. Her wrists were tied, and a mantle bound around her head stopped her mouth.

"But what is to happen to her?" asked one of the men.

"I bring her here to her marriage," the nobleman proclaimed, "and if you knew the power of her bridegroom, you would not dare question me. You know that many years ago, my fortunes declined sharply when a fleet of ships were lost at sea. It was then I came to this cursed isle and promised my daughter Isabella to the sea spirit who dwells here in return for better fortune. Indeed, my wealth then increased. But the night before the wedding, this slattern ran away. More ships were lost and my lands withered! In desperation I offered up my bastard child, my wife's maid, to the spirit, but he would not have her. Now, after years of living in disgrace as an actress, at last this fool has returned to Venice. The sea spirit shall finally have her, and my fortunes shall be restored!"

I could stand to hear no more from this greedy, diabolical man. With more anger than planning, I rushed into the room, mask still on and prop sword held high.

"Demon!" I called, "release her!"

Everyone looked at me in astonishment.

"Who is this?" asked Isabella's father.

"It is an actor from your daughter's troupe," said one of the men.

"You're wrong!" I declared, making my voice sound as confident as possible. "I am no mere actor. How do you think I got here so quickly? I flew in my magical chariot." With my sword, I gestured to the men holding Isabella. "If you three know what is good for you, you will release her at once. For I am a true spirit, much stronger than whatever this sorry excuse for a father is aligned with."

Isabella motioned desperately to the men to free her mouth, and one acquiesced.

"Though you wrong me, listen to him," she begged the men, clasping her bound hands to her breast. "He is too powerful a creature for you to vex. When we were in France, he burned an entire village's fruit trees to the ground just by blinking. Their only crime was to mock me on the stage. Imagine what he will do to you for stealing me. For you see, he considers us—" She broke off for a moment, sending an anguished, heartrending glance in my direction. "—married!"

Never had I been so grateful for a mask, for I was sure the surprise would show on my face otherwise. Nonetheless, I built off her brilliant suggestion.

"Yes, she is my wife," I said proudly. "I wed her in a secret ceremony at the top of Monte Bianco. Our vows were written in the blood of a phoenix."

The men were transfixed, their grip on her slackening.

"It's true," Isabella said, tears streaming down her cheeks. "If you do not let me go, you sentence me not only to be the bride of a sea monster...but to commit the sin of bigamy!"

With that, she executed a flawless swoon, and the men scrambled to catch her.

"Lies!" yelled Isabella's father. "Lies and nonsense! I doubt this loudmouth youth has any magic at all."

"You doubt me?" I cried. "I doubt your stories of this sea spirit.

Perhaps you were drunk, and actually promised your daughter to a fish."

Isabella's father became florid with rage. "It is real, and dangerous! My wife can attest! She saw the creature when I offered up her maid Pampinea as substitute. Tell them!"

Here he gestured to the sobbing woman, but she was distraught beyond reason.

"Please spare her," she cried—whether to her husband or me I could not tell. "Please spare my daughter!"

Isabella's mother fell from the chair to her knees, her black skirts spread around her like a pit of despair.

"Look how you have upset my poor mother-in-law," I scolded. "Men, if you doubt me, go outside and see for yourself that there is no boat I could have arrived in. Who will you trust? This cruel man, or me?" (Here, I did a neat flourish with my sword.)

The men stood thunderstruck for a moment, and then one took it upon himself to start undoing Isabella's bonds, and the others joined in. My heart soared. Freed, Isabella ran into my arms, and I held her as tightly to my bound bosom as I could.

"You idiots!" cried her father. "You will doom us all!"

"Don't you harm them."

It was the voice of Pierrot! Our company and the young woman who had cried out to warn Isabella rushed into the room.

"We are not too late!" exclaimed the young woman.

"Pampinea!" Isabella cried.

"Ah, the rest of our troupe has arrived," I said. "Because they are not magic, like me, they could not fly here."

I hoped my colleagues would not question this, but before anyone could, there was a sound like the wailing of a storm, and heavy footsteps descended the steps of the tower.

"It comes to claim its bride!" exclaimed Isabella's father triumphantly.

I can hardly relate what it was that came down those stairs. It was in the shape of a man, but oh—his skin! It was of scales, and the color of a drowned corpse. Along his arms were sapphire fins with barbed points. More alarmingly, he was naked, save for a crown of seashells from which seaweed hung. When he reached the last stair, he gazed ominously at those of us gathered. Terror struck my heart, and yet I raised my sword again as Isabella hid her face against my neck.

Isabella's father dropped to his knees. "Honored master," he said, "powerful spirit who holds my fortunes in his hand. Look, I have at last brought you what I promised: your bride, my daughter Isabella."

The sea spirit focused his gaze on the woman in my arms.

"My wife is not for the taking," I said firmly.

"Your wife?" the creature hissed, displaying its teeth of sea urchin spines.

"Yes, my wife," I attested. "This untrustworthy man would have you play cuckold, trying to marry you to a woman already wed."

The creature glared at Isabella's father, rage in its eyes.

"Fool!" it growled. "You have failed yet again to bring me what you promised, and not only that, you have brought a crowd of strangers to my sacred isle. I rue the day I struck a deal with you."

"I apologize for the unexpected guests, noble spirit," I said graciously, bowing. "With your permission, myself, my wife, and our friends will leave at once."

To my surprise, the creature nodded. "Go. Go all of you, and never return! As for this useless acolyte," he said, gesturing to Isabella's father, "I take his life in revenge!"

Isabella's father cried out, but it was too late. With superhuman speed, the creature pounced and dragged him from the tower and into the sea.

* * *

There was a touching reunion between Isabella and her mother, and then we boarded our makeshift fleet to return to Venice. During this journey, much was explained by Pampinea, the maid who had been revealed to be Isabella's half-sister. When Pampinea was but twelve years old, her mother, a laundress, died, and she was left to her nobleman father. The immoral and selfish man wanted nothing to do with his illegitimate child, but gave her to his wife as a maid, meaning to mock her with a constant reminder of his infidelity. Instead, Isabella's mother came to love her step-daughter.

On the morning of our performance, Pampinea overheard her father's plans to have his men try once again to kidnap Isabella, after they had failed to bring her from the Duke's palazzo. Having seen the sea spirit herself when she had been offered to the creature, Pampinea begged him to relent. Her father was furious and locked her in a room, telling his wife that if she said a word to anyone, he would kill Pampinea after disposing of their daughter.

Pampinea, however, refused to give up. Summoning all of her courage, she broke a window, climbed down the wall, and raced to our performance space, arriving just a moment too late. After I ran off in pursuit of Isabella, she told the rest of our troupe of her father's insidious plan and led them to the island.

"Oh, brave sister!" cried Isabella. "I never even knew until today you were my sister, and yet you risked all for me! And Flaminia! How brave and clever you were!"

"And now," sighed Isabella's mother, "though it might be a sin to rejoice at the death of my husband, I at last know my daughter and my step-daughter are safe from his schemes."

She clasped both ladies in her arms, and I realized then that Isabella could remain in Venice with her mother and newfound sister. As happy as I was for the three women, grief struck my heart like an arrow from Despair itself.

The most difficult acting performance of my life took place that night, when I forced myself to look glad during our celebratory dinner, which I feared marked the beginning of the end of my companionship with Isabella. Perhaps she would move into her family's palazzo immediately, rather than continue to room with us. She loved acting, so I hoped she would not quit our shows while we remained in Venice, but after that? How I longed for a mask! Although I felt I was giving a good show, Isabella took my arm and led me into a hallway.

"My cunning hero, what is the matter?" she asked.

"Oh, Isabella," I said, my voice breaking, "It is right and proper that you are reunited with your mother and sister, but I grieve, for surely now you will stay in Venice."

Then, to my shock and joy, the arrow launched by Despair was struck aside by one from Cupid, for Isabella stopped my mouth with a kiss.

"Beloved Flaminia," she said, "will you quit me so soon after declaring me your wife? I am of course elated to be reunited with my mother and sister, but how could I leave you? If you will have me, I will be yours forever."

Sometime later we had our own ceremony as we traveled between cities, with Pierrot as officiant and the rest of the company as attendants and witnesses. We were passing through a lonely little valley at the time, but our hearts felt higher than the Alps.

Fittonia

Libby Feltis

Libby Feltis is a bisexual woman living in the country with her family, two tiny dogs, and an ever-growing number of chickens. When she's not busy writing, she can be found trying to talk to the crows.

November

"Five, four, three, two, one...You may open your eyes now."

Toni didn't want to leave the solitude of her dreamscape. This time Sebastian had taken her to a beach, empty save for an emerald-green chair whose velvet upholstery begged her to sit. There were no birds needing to be fed, no phones to be answered, and no pictures to be taken to prove to the insurance company that a tornado had in fact demolished her home. Just Toni, the lapping waves of the ocean, and her chest rising and falling to the rhythm.

"How did that feel?" he asked when she finally lifted one eyelid.

"It felt"—she sighed—"like a place that doesn't exist." She pried the other eyelid open with a forceful finger.

"But it exists in your mind now. Which means you can return there whenever you need to."

"Even without your"—Toni gestured at Sebastian—"magic shit."

"Even without being hypnotized, yes."

Toni doubted that. She'd be lucky if she made it back to her government issued FEMA trailer without flipping someone off.

Serenity wasn't in her vocabulary, never mind her demeanor. She was angry, yes. Sad, sure. Discontent, maybe. Horny, usually. But serene? Let's just say no one had ever mistaken her for someone who practiced yoga and drank chamomile tea. Everything about her read: coffee, black; whiskey, neat; car horn, activated; music, loud; opinion, given; language, foul; jacket, leather; mother, single.

"I'm not the only magic one in this room," Sebastian said, peering over her so that he looked upside down.

"Someone should really do something about the gossip in this town," Toni said.

Sebastian smirked and playfully smacked her on the arm.

"Life will get easier soon."

"It could hurry the hell up!" She sat up, put her coat on, and handed Sebastian an envelope. "One session for one story, as promised."

Toni left the hypnosis office thinking about the irony of two people trading modalities to reframe their lives and the ways they thought about them. It was as if their magic only worked for other people. As the town's hypnotist and resident witch writer, they were destined to be friends. Sebastian had been helping her tap into the calm part of her mind since everything imploded last spring. In exchange, she had been writing him an intuitive short story—a slow burn romance between him and the man he hadn't met yet. Toni couldn't look at Sebastian without scenes of domestic bliss and dachshund puppies filling her mind. The latest chapter detailed his first kiss with the mystery man. She hoped it would fill him with hope, anticipation, and the openness to manifest the Mr. to his Mr.

Whether or not she could have an easier life was another thing. Maybe if her parents had named her something other than Fittonia. Fittonia! The plant that needs just enough but not too much sunlight or it'll faint. It requires watering but too few drops and it turns brown. Three drops too many and, you guessed it, it faints. Too cold? Withers. Too warm? Withers. It's a high maintenance plant that thrives on being ignored and only being tended to in its hour of need—whenever that might be. Oh, and its surroundings needed to be just right—whatever that meant. Fittonia: nicknamed the nerve plant by botanists.

Toni Chandler's surroundings were never just right. She was as finicky and affected by everything as the plant her hippie-boomer parents named her after. Things rarely went right for Toni. Meanwhile, they had named her golden-haired sister Forsythia—after a hardy bush that bloomed gold every spring without fail. It didn't matter if the world was falling down around Sita, because she knew that every spring her luck would shift. She'd land an unexpected promotion with a private office and significant pay raise. The extra ten pounds she'd put on in the winter months would vanish overnight, and she'd walk around like fucking Vanna White, smile smugly in place.

Toni's namesake didn't bloom golden, it veined silver. So, despite being the younger sister, her dark hair had gray strands lacing through its long waves. If Sita was Jane Eyre, then Toni was Bertha Mason; she looked less like a woman men fell in love with and more like the crazed wife they kept in the attic so that she didn't burn the place down. At least her parents hadn't named her Bertha.

Names mattered. You couldn't convince Toni otherwise. While Sita wore hers like a May Day crown, Toni carried hers like a heavily guarded curse. Sensitive didn't begin to describe the level of empathy she had been saddled with. And unlike their entrepreneurial father, Toni had yet to figure out how to make her intuition work for her. It felt more like an allergy to the world than the spiritual gift their witchy family insisted it was. She was approaching forty and no closer to cracking the code than she'd been at ten when she realized other people's temperatures, their moods, their thoughts, changed her leaves. They made her wither or rise.

***

When Toni got home, the crows were waiting. After the tornado had taken—no that made it sound too gentle. After the tornado murdered her chickens with the tree it smashed into their coop, she found herself still going out to feed them every morning. A few days later, the crows showed up and began eating the mealworms she'd mechanically throw out because the muscle memory of the chore wouldn't leave her. They had been gone for a week and Toni had assumed they'd found greener pasture—someone somewhere reeling them in with shiny gifts. But today they were back, and she felt pathetic for being relieved.

Toni reached into the pocket of her leather jacket and threw out a handful of sunflower seeds onto the driveway. The sun had begun to set already, because even North Carolina autumns waited for no one. Just then a hawk flew over the trailer, causing the bravest of the crows to squawk and fly off after him. Toni checked the mailbox, which had managed to weather the storm. The metal door creaked as she opened it, and pinpricks climbed the back of Toni's neck. *Shit, a hawk.* Always a sign of change for her. She had seen a hawk fly over the house the evening before the tornado.

"That's right! Go on, git! Ya shit bird."

The mailbox offered its gifts: an energy bill (*rude*), coupons for an oil change (*who had the time?*), and an official looking envelope with a return address from a lawyer in New York. Toni's stomach sank. She ran-walked to the trailer, flinging its flimsy door open when she reached it. Fred's beak thudded against the glass just as the door closed behind her. *Oops.* She would let him in after she read the letter. She began tearing through the envelope as carefully as her trembling hands would let her. *Tap, tap, tap.* He was at the kitchen window now.

"Jesus, Fred. Give me a minute!" she called over her shoulder, her eyes scanning through the legalese. Fred: a wise name, for a wise animal. *Wise ass*, as she affectionately called him.

"Mom!" Anson called from his room. Just fifteen, his voice was already lower than his father's—a fact she liked to bring up to her ex-husband, Donovan, whenever possible.

"Don't tell me you're hungry, dude. You know how to microwave—"

"No, Mom. Look," he said in his flat, impatient way.

Toni looked up as Anson walked into the kitchen with Fred on his shoulder. He was pretending to be annoyed, but she saw the amusement in his eyes. Toni had named Anson so that he had zero plant complications. Anson: meaning Ann's son, or the son of the divine. She didn't know who Ann was, but it was a common enough name that she hoped her son wouldn't inherit her bad luck. Being the son of Ann or the divine had to be better than being the son of Fittonia Chandler. The tornado had been the ultimate evidence of that truth. Sometimes she believed they'd survived just to struggle more. If anything could undo two overly sensitive people, it was living in a metal box which swayed when the wind picked up.

"He was tapping on my window with this." Anson held up a

silver house key. So, he had found someone with shiny gifts. At least he came back.

"Traitor," she murmured to the bird when he hopped off Anson's shoulder and onto the kitchen counter where the letter lay unread. Anson placed the key on the counter, too. Then he went to the cupboard where they kept the sunflower seeds and presented a small pile of them to the bird. Toni went back to reading the letter.

"This makes no sense," she said.

"What is it?"

"It's a copy of Aunt Hel's last will and testament. It says she's left her house in Fall Creek to me, but she isn't even—"

Just then her phone rang, DAD flashing across the caller ID.

"Fuck," Toni said as she swiped to answer the call. *Sorry*, she mouthed to Anson, who shrugged.

"Nice to talk to you, too," her father said as she brought the phone to her ear.

"Aunt Hel's dead, isn't she?" There was a pause before he answered. Toni met eyes with Anson and exchanged looks that said, *another day, another loss*. Their favorite people, chickens, and places were crumbling around them.

"Yes, honey, she is. I always knew you two were in tune, but this is uncanny."

"No, it's not, Dad," Toni huffed. "I just read her last will and testament, and there's a crow on my counter with a key in his mouth." Fred had picked the key back up and was inching toward her, his flat feet flip-flopping in a way that was too cute for the moment. *Time and place, Fred.* She pinched the bridge of her nose, closed her eyes, and warded off the tears.

"She was always efficient. Had impeccable timing. I guess this is no exception," she heard her father reasoning. He was an infuriating optimist. Everything happened for a reason if you asked Orin Chandler. Toni opened her eyes and scanned the FEMA trailer. There were so few things of their own. Anson's dad had replaced his video game console and all his games in lieu of showing up. Donovan, the whole reason they ended up living in North Carolina in the first place. Donovan: a name meaning darkness. He had certainly brought darkness to several years of Toni's life. Being present wasn't his strong suit.

Now what was left for them in this place but hostility and regret? Even Anson's formerly small school had grown to the point of congestion. Her fifteen-year-old was coming home every day looking as tired and overstimulated as she felt. The whole situation felt like wearing a sweater that no longer fit; it scratched in places and restricted their movement. There was little left to make this place feel like home. What scant family photos Toni had before digital times had been lost in the tornado. The lack of history, of an anchor, made her feel like a ghost floating through rooms that didn't belong to her.

"Did you know about this? The house?"

"With Beth gone, who else would she leave it to?" Her father had a way of not exactly answering questions.

"I don't know. Maybe Sita?"

"Even if Helena had died in the spring, she would have still left the house to you. Your sister's good luck can't trump an aunt's favoritism."

"Ha! So, you admit you gave Sita the better name. It's about time, old man."

"No, but I know that's what you believe. Anyway, no funeral—"

"Because Aunt Hel wanted to be burned and planted with a tree next to Aunt Beth."

"Precisely. On the land that you now own. Sounds like you inherited the crows as well."

Toni hadn't made the connection until now. The crows had shown up after she had told her aunt about the chickens and the tornado. If anyone knew how to keep a Fittonia alive, it was Aunt Hel, and now she was gone, too. Toni ended the call with her dad and sunk down onto her elbows, tears betraying her with each *plop, plop* onto the counter. Anson's hand was on her back, rubbing circles in a rare gesture of affection. After a moment, she straightened, pushing her frizzing hair away from her face.

"How do you feel about us going to Fall Creek for a little while?"

"What? And leave all this?" Anson gestured to a cabinet door that was hanging by one hinge. Toni smiled.

"Has anyone ever told you that your spiritual gift is sarcasm?"

"Has anyone ever told you that yours is swearing?"

"Go pack your shit. Let's get the hell out of here, kid."

Anson smiled then, for the first time in months.

December

Toni was surprised by how easy it was to leave North Carolina. It was as if she and Anson had run out of tears for the place by the time they rolled out of there. She even managed to keep her middle fingers on the wheel and only hit the horn twice. It helped that the crows followed their moving truck up the east coast back to their original home. "Home." It was the first thing out of both of their mouths as they stepped through the door of the American Gothic cottage. Toni stomped the snow off her black combat boots.

"I call dibs on the attic room," Anson said, climbing up the stairs two at a time with his long legs.

She ran her hand along the lime washed walls before turning into the den. Family photos lined the walls in gold frames. Someone had already laid logs and kindling in the woodstove, so all Toni had to do was strike a match and throw it in. Sinking down into one of the two emerald wingback chairs, she watched the flames lap at the wood. It was hypnotic, taking her back to the last time she had visited her aunt. Toni had rubbed at her eyes that evening, smudging her mascara. Aunt Hel noticed.

"I'm not a painted woman—anymore. In my twenties I would rouge my cheeks and cat-eye my liner until every angle was sharp. I wanted my cheekbones to seem different from the broad Austrian features I was born with. Roundness, you see, was not an option. Not if you were going to trap a man.

"No, only sharpness could do that, could snag one on the impossible knife of a jawline, the blade of a collarbone. And so, I painted my oval face into a diamond."

"What happened?" Toni had asked, examining her aunt's features.

"I caught your Aunt Beth instead." Toni remembered how the

corners of her aunt's thin mouth slowly curved up into a reluctant smile.

"You miss her."

"More than you know."

Then they each sipped their whiskey and watched the fog creep up from the valley.

"I can't do wing tipped eyeliner. The closer I get to forty, the more hooded my eyes get," Toni had said. Aunt Hel peered at her from the farthest corner of her good eye.

"You won't need to."

"What's that supposed to mean?" Jesus, even then, her aunt had sensed her imminent spinsterhood. That's probably why she left the house to Toni, to keep her distracted while her vagina dried up and sealed itself shut.

"I mean, it's not gonna matter what your make-up looks like. He's not going to care."

"Who's not going to care?"

Aunt Hel had just squinted at the fog, like she was seeing something much further away—something that wasn't there at all—something in the future. They had this gift in common, though Toni had stopped trying to intuit her own future sometime after her divorce. Instead, her magic turned outward, sensing things about everyone around her. Grocery shopping was an exercise in insanity. She was a radio tuned into every frequency. Different voices, thoughts, visions, feelings, and memories overwhelmed her—none of them her own. Instacart had been an answer to her witch prayers. She couldn't remember the last time she stepped inside a busy store. She hoped they'd deliver out to Fall Creek.

Something poked Toni's side as she shifted to cross her legs, taking her out of her thoughts. She rooted around in the crack between the seat cushion and arm, pulling out a planner dated for the new year. Every week had already been filled out. Who planned their entire year before Yule? Helena Chandler, that's who. Aunt Hel's meticulousness bordered on eccentricity. Still, as Toni scanned through the first week of January, she realized her aunt had mastered the art of intentional living. January 1: *Take cookies to the neighbors.* January 3: *Book group at library, 7pm.* January 5: *Aikido at the community center, 9am.* January 7: *Register Anson for school at Finger Lakes Charter.*

"Wait. What?" Toni flipped to the first page of the planner, and there in her aunt's precise script was written, *The Care and Feeding of Fittonia Chandler.*

January

Toni followed the planner over the next several weeks. Aunt Hel was careful to never overschedule a week. She left a day of rest between every day with an activity. 'Neighbor' was a loose term in Fall Creek. The closest house was two acres away, and its occupant was a stocky, single farmer who gazed at Toni like he was looking for a Bertha Mason to shake things up. After she brought him cookies, he could be found plowing her driveway even on days it didn't snow. Toni was enjoying the consistency as much as the view.

If Tractor Supply was handing out awards for best dressed farm hand, this man would have won. His Carhartt pants were caked in the seasons—the mud of spring, grass stains of summer, and salt residue of winter ringed the cuffs. Had they ever been washed? No, Toni decided, they had not. And Harris wore the dirt like a badge. Above them was a threadbare thermal, framed by the blue and green plaid flannel she'd come to spot him by. Her eyes scanned up to his scot-red beard, not to be confused with that patchy ginger monstrosity Donovan was always trying to grow. This was the beard of a man who could spend the night in the bush just to wake at dawn and strangle a buck with his bare hands. A hunter-gatherer beard. But that's not what Toni said when she caught herself staring.

"Fucking hipster potato farmers," she grumbled. "None of you know how to park."

"Is that what you say to everyone who voluntarily plows your driveway with their tractor?" Harris asked.

"Is that a euphemism?"

"Is that an offer?"

Toni opened her mouth and closed it. Now Harris was wearing her speechlessness as a badge of honor. Toni cleared her throat and kicked at the icicles that were hanging off her tailgate.

"I never asked you to plow my driveway."

"Are you complaining? Because I can put all the snow back if you'd like." He turned on the heel of his insulated Muck boot.

"No, you can't," Toni said, calling his bluff. "I just watched you get that thing stuck in the ditch. Must be too small"—she paused—"or perhaps too big to get the job done." She let her gaze drop to his pants before meeting his eyes again. His face blushed wildly. "Your cheeks are burning."

"I swear, Fittonia Chandler, you could light my house on fire and I think I'd still ask you out to dinner," Harris said, shaking his head.

"I just might let you."

***

Meanwhile, the book club turned out to be less book and more club—soda mixed with vodka and lime. The members showed up in varying degrees of black dress, and Toni in her leather jacket and combat boots felt in context for the first time in her life. These people had their own magic. The members bitched, burned the names of their foes in the library fireplace, swapped tarot readings, and talked about their favorite books. Often, they shared fond memories of Helena and Beth. A few of them approached Toni after the first meeting and asked about her intuitive short stories.

"Hel said you charge $125 per chapter, and that if we tried to low ball you, she'd haunt us."

"Oh, um..." Toni had never charged for her stories before. She'd only bartered or given them as gifts.

Witchcraft had become mainstream, cute, something to dabble in or make money from just like everything else in this capitalist country. But to Toni it wasn't something she could pick up and set down like the crystals at a Body, Mind, Spirit Expo. It was more like the birthmark on the inside of her arm; she could hide it, but it didn't go away. And sometimes, in direct light, it itched. The gifts passed down to her begged to be used, but if she didn't? Chaos. Unused magic got restless and made its own messes—much like the food expiring in the back of her fridge. She had to find a way to keep her magic occupied, purring, instead of meowing in heat. It was almost impossible when trying to live a normal life, one where her wavy hair was considered exotic and not akin to Medusa.

Toni's online copyediting job hardly stirred her creative juices nor quelled her magic. So, her intuitive short stories became a kind of salve—a way for her to use her magic for good. They were the spells for those who felt stuck, a way to ignite their imagination. Until now, it was a well-kept secret that almost all her stories came true for the recipients. Whatever they said they wanted to change would manifest after they read the story she wrote. Maybe that's why she'd never written one for herself; she hadn't known where to begin mending the mess. She didn't trust her intuition when it came to herself.

"Just take the money, dear," Mrs. Jenks said, pressing it into her hand. "I'll email you the details. Helena gave us all your card before she passed."

Toni didn't have cards, but Mrs. Jenks was flashing a black business card at her with the name *Fittonia Chandler* embossed in gold.

***

Sebastian called that evening to let her know he'd met someone.

"You sound different," he said. "You haven't even asked me his name."

"Does it matter?"

"To me? No. But I would have thought you'd want to look it up, just in case."

Toni thought about this for a moment and realized she hadn't even looked up Harris's name after his offer to grab dinner sometime. Either she was slipping, or she was getting soft. She blamed the Aikido lessons.

Aikido is a Japanese martial art which focuses on redirecting your opponent's energy rather than cultivating violence or aggression. It helps extra-sensory people filter unwanted energy as well. After a month of lessons, Toni could walk into public without her protective leather jacket on. She wasn't immune to her intuition now, but she could turn it down and that made grocery shopping feel less like the seventh circle of hell. Her hyper-vigilance wasn't ruling her life.

"I've met someone, too," she admitted.

"Is his name Tom?"

"No. Why do you ask?"

"Because that's the name of the guy I'm going out with this weekend."

"Tom sounds like a nice name."

"You mean generic," Sebastian accused.

"I mean, maybe names aren't the curses I've made them out to be."

"Oh," he clucked. "He must be hot."

"Hot, consistent, good with a snowplow," Toni listed.

"Is that a euphemism?"

"It's about to be."

"Now, there's the Fittonia I know and love."

February

Anson found his pod at Finger Lakes Charter. Turns out there were a lot of witches with quirky kids in this part of New York. Here his autism wasn't treated as a diagnosis to overcome but as a superpower that needed honing. Toni began filling in a planner for after school let out. She titled it *The Care and Feeding of Anson O'Leary.* In it, she wrote things like, "Play Dungeons and Dragons with friends from school," and "Take a walk with Fred on the trails behind our house."

"Our house" was the only way Anson referred to the home they'd inherited. There was no question of returning to North Carolina. When Toni broached the subject with him, he said, "And leave all this?" But this time he was smiling with Fred on his shoulder and a phone lighting up in his hand with texts from the new friends he'd made. "I gotta go, Mom. We're playing video games online in five minutes!"

"Is Fred playing, too?" she called after him as he took the stairs two at a time up to his room.

"Fred is my good luck charm," he yelled back. "He gave us the key to this house."

***

February was a busy month. Toni's days were filled with writing stories for her aunt's friends and whoever they would hand her card to. She even made a website so that people could order intuitive short stories from her. Now she was incorporating tarot readings, spells, and other witchy things she'd picked up from the ladies at book group. (Weren't all book groups just a coven in disguise?) And although she wasn't ready to admit it yet, the story Toni had begun writing for herself featured a love interest not unlike Harris the hipster potato farmer. She hoped he'd still like her when he found out she was a witch. Something told her she could write that into being. Half the magic—she'd come to realize—was in the belief that her stories could come true.

Toni began believing good things for herself, for her name and what it meant.

When the planner's page showed February 13th, Toni received a text from Sebastian.

S: *Tom invited me out for Valentine's Day!*

T: *Ask him how he feels about dachshunds.*

S: *You witch, you.*

The next text was a picture of Sebastian's mystery man holding a dachshund. Toni smiled and then checked the planner for that day's activity. She frowned when she read the words: *Dust the plant stand in your bathroom.* But she was learning to trust the process.

The bathroom was where Aunt Hel kept her one and only Fittonia plant on a stand next to the clawfoot tub. The plant seemed to be thriving there in the dappled light of the frosted glass window, so Toni hadn't moved it. A task was a task, though. So, she picked up the pot from the plant stand. As she did, a folded piece of paper fell to the floor. It read: *Fittonia's are easy. Sometimes they just need to be repotted.*

Kryvoye Lake

Oksana Marafioti

Oksana Marafioti is a BIPOC writer of Romani, Armenian, and Ukrainian descent. Her memoir, American Gypsy, was published in 2012 by FSG. Oksana has published essays, poems, and stories in Time, Slate, The Rumpus, LA Times, storySouth, Literary Orphans, Pilgrimage, and several anthologies, including Immigrant Voices (Penguin, 2015). She was the 2013 Library of Congress Fellow and the 2020 Picador Guest Fellow at the University of Leipzig, Germany. Currently, Oksana is working on her second memoir about transgenerational trauma, identity, and belonging, for which she has received a 2022 grant from the National Endowment For the Arts. Connect with Oksana here: https://www.oksana-marafioti.com/

There once lived a young Romani man plagued by a love for two Romani women.

Every morning he would rise and think, *Today, I will choose. The beautiful Darya or the industrious Marina.* And every night, sated by Darya's love and Marina's cooking, he would go to bed undecided.

Soon, the maidens insisted he accept one of them for his wife. The villagers were beginning to talk, and gossip could not be afforded in a place where the difference between happiness and exile rested in one's reputation. Ivan had little choice but to let one love go.

The night he carried his mother's old betrothal ring to his bride's door, the moon shepherded him with a vigilant glow, and in the distance, the wind picked at the surface of the lake Ivan fished every day. Along with Ivan, the moon and the wind seemed to fret. Could he truly commit his heart where it had split in two for so very long? To the left, on the other side of the lake, lay Darya's hut, carved into an ancient oak rumored to hold the mystical powers of her sorcerer ancestors. Marina's log house stood in the square to the right. Built by her merchant father out of the sturdiest of pines, its grand design and an iron ridgepole, topped with the family's insignia, identified the dwelling as the fanciest in the countryside.

What can a fisherman's son do, Ivan thought, *if not try and better his station?*

***

The wedding was a grand affair as such things go. Marina's father loosened his pockets until the tables groaned under the mouth-watering dishes his wife and daughter created for the occasion. Drink was plentiful and company boisterous. Music sprung from *balalaika* strings while the bards entertained the crowd with tales of devils and fairies.

Marina made the perfect hostess. With the grace of a swan, she glided across the room, poured *Medovukha* into goblets and attended to every guest as if they were royalty. Upon seeing this, pride bloomed in Ivan's chest, for he knew he had made the right choice.

That night joy abounded, and all believed it would stay for a while.

But the very next day, the church bells rang the frantic rhythm of tragedy.

Darya had gone missing.

A party searched the woods, but three days later the men returned to work and Darya, being a witch's daughter, was quickly forgotten.

The very next day Ivan too resumed his duties, leaving Marina to tend the house. When he began to prepare his boat he discovered his lucky net was gone, and his mood, already sour, blackened.

Bad luck for a fisherman, the other men said. But Ivan dismissed their superstitions, borrowed a spare and pushed on.

In the middle of the lake, as Ivan minded the net, murky thoughts pulled him under. Where had Darya gone? Could she not see why he had to choose Marina? If she loved him, why would she run away? He was mad at her for acting childish, but he also missed her fiercely.

Behind the Earth, the sun had fallen by the time Ivan tugged his boat up the banks of the lake. The moonless night reeked of algae, the calls of frogs and crickets piercing through the fog. A shadow separated from a nearby willow tree, and Ivan strained to see it approach.

"Darya? Darya. Is it really you?"

The woman stepped closer, her outline black for the lack of a moon. She raised a hand as if to touch Ivan's face, but stilled.

"Ivanushka. My love. How could you marry another?" she asked.

He frowned, resolute not to show any indication of self-pity he had suffered moments earlier. "Is that why you ran like the devil was after you? Leave it up to you to act so foolish."

"But I had to get away from the sounds of your wedding, far enough to not hear anything."

Ivan gave her a stern look. She wore a dress with long wide sleeves and a hem stitched in gold thread. It made him smile. The dress was a gift he had brought her from a fair a year ago. Her hair fell down her back in a thick braid so heavy even the wind strained to pick at it, and though Ivan could not discern her features, his fingers begged to touch her delicate skin. Once his thoughts drifted, Ivan reminded himself that he was a married man now and his mind was a stone bridge, unmovable even by the strongest of urges.

"We can be no more, Darya. Go home. My wife is waiting."

He began to walk up the bank toward the village and for a moment, it seemed she would heed. But then he heard soft footsteps and half-turned to see her, head bowed like that of an obedient child.

"I said go," he grumbled.

"But there is nothing for me without you."

And Darya followed Ivan until he climbed the steps of his house. She stood at the bottom and did not move, not even when he disappeared inside.

For two days, not a moment clean of doubt escaped Ivan. Had he wed the right girl? Meanwhile, Marina bustled around the kitchen and tossed furtive glances and smiles at him as she kneaded the dough for the Apple Baba pie. Whenever Ivan caught her looking, she blushed, taking him back to the last few nights, when she had proven her talents did not end at the ovens.

But no sooner did Ivan close his mind to Darya than she appeared again. The lake was a miser that day. Ever since the net had vanished, he had no luck catching fish, and after ten hours of breaking surface Ivan's barrel held but four puny carp.

Darya wrung her hands and waited for him to leave the boat. Her dress was muddy at the bottom, and strands of hair escaped her braid.

"Why haven't you gone home?" Ivan asked.

"There is no home without you." Her voice trembled, as did her body. She hugged herself and gestured at the water. "My love for you would overflow this lake. My tears fill it even as I confess, and they will break its banks one day."

Mesmerized, Ivan met Darya's sorrowful gaze, and even in the dark, the sheen in her eyes was unmistakable. An urge to comfort her nearly flew him to her side. Instead, Ivan heaved the fish barrel over one shoulder to distract himself. "What is this witchery, woman? You must let me be."

Darya dipped one hand into the lake, and rising, held it out to him. "You can taste the salt if you wish."

Only then did Ivan's senses return. "It's a freshwater lake, little fool."

"No longer."

"Why can't you understand?" he muttered through his teeth. "I am with Marina now."

The shudder was gone from her body, and she lifted her face like a queen before her subject.

"Look past the false bliss you've wrapped yourself in. I'm here because you want me still."

And no matter how Ivan searched for denial, none came forth.

"Marina's waiting," he finally managed and strode away.

"And so am I." The wind carried to Ivan's ears before he disappeared around the corner.

He rushed home to find solace, but even in bed, next to Marina, the night offered little peace. Outside, the wind bellowed and whipped the roofs of the houses. And inside, each time poor Ivan closed his eyes, Darya beckoned. The woman had climbed his walls like ivy, clasped unto his newly hatched contentment with her merciless vines. He wanted nothing more than to feel satisfied with his life. Yet beneath Ivan's rebellion against Darya's persistence, his weakness for both her and Marina unexpectedly overwhelmed him.

Sitting up on the edge of the bed, Ivan brooded like the wind chasing absolution down the empty road. And with Darya back, it had become clear only one thing would bring it about.

To possess both women.

***

Ivan set out for the lake, his feet not his own, his heart aflame. It took but a moment to locate Darya waiting, as he predicted, near the boat. She rushed to him.

"Ivanushka!"

"I was a foolish man," he exclaimed, clasping her hands in his.

To this she smiled and kissed his knuckles, and he noticed how cold she felt to his touch.

"You need a fire."

"And now you're here, my dear Ivan," she said.

"Let us go home."

"You mean you will stay?"

When Ivan nodded, Darya threw her arms around him, pressing her cheek to his chest. The dampness of her dress seeped through his shirt.

Pulling her after him, Ivan untied the rope that tethered his boat to the shore. "You need warmth before you catch your death. Come. We will celebrate our reunion in your soft feather bed," he said, marveling at his own idiocy. Why had he ever thought this would be difficult?

Obediently, Darya entered the boat and sat across from Ivan, who began to row with great long strokes fortified with pride. Darya traced her fingers in the water, giggling whenever their eyes met. But the closer they approached the lake's heart, the more wicked Darya's laughter grew until it resembled her voice not at all. At first Ivan assumed she had caught a cold and was now in fits of a fever. If he touched her forehead, it would surely be burning.

"Calm yourself, angel heart," he said, rowing faster. No one has ever found the bottom of Krivoye Lake, and it was rumored to be teeming with giant fish, monsters that could swallow a grown man. Though not a fool for old wives' tales, Ivan had no desire to find out for himself.

She splashed him with a playful wink.

"Darya. Enough."

Again she splashed. Ivan yanked the paddles inside the boat and stood, but she never ceased her games, taken by some kind of a spell.

"Don't be afraid of a little water, Ivanushka. It is not as cold as it seems."

"Why should I be afraid?"

At that, Darya rose in one fluid motion. "Then take off your clothes," she said with an unsettling urgency, "and swim with me."

Ivan stole a glance at the lake he had fished since childhood, but hastily turned away. It yawned like the maw of a sinkhole.

"What is with you?" he asked. "I am to blame for making you wait, I know this much. But I'm here now, and my only wish is to take you home and keep you safe."

An eerie silence descended. No trace of the wind, no song of the night creatures. Only water licking at the boat's ribs.

A long, silvery tear slid down Darya's cheek, and finally, after three days, the moon reappeared from behind the clouds.

Ivan beheld Darya's face and staggered back to the boat's edge. More tears escaped her. Only now, with the moonlight bright, Ivan glimpsed the truth. Not tears, but tiny fish wriggled out of the corners of Darya's milky eyes. One by one, they plopped to the deck at her bare feet.

She cocked her head at the lake, her once beautiful face bloated and tinged blue. "This is my home now. This is my bed."

Darya stripped off her dress and there, wrapped around her throat, stretched against her skin, was Ivan's lucky net. Right below, a wicked gash claimed the expanse of Darya's abdomen. From it, beasts of all kinds slithered and crawled; crabs pinching their claws, newts scurrying faster than a blink, and water bugs swarming out in such numbers that the deck began to breathe around Ivan.

"I don't believe you," he said. "Nobody saw you on the lake that day. You, you, your body would've floated up." He covered his face. "What am I saying? This is mad."

"All it took was a few large rocks to drag me under. I hardly felt it. But I heard your voice calling, begging me to come and take you away."

Darya advanced and the smell of algae intensified threefold.

"You promised you would come home with me, Ivan," she said, inches away, her breath stale and rusty. Before Ivan's very eyes, her skin began to wither.

"I'm sorry," he said. The only escape was to jump, yet a conviction that his own death lurked kept Ivan fixed in place. "For what I've done. To you. I am so sorry."

"Let me take you home."

When Darya's lips touched Ivan's, he shivered to his toes, then, before he could defeat his panic, the maiden dragged him overboard. They were gone with nary a splash and the lake shut the world out of its tomb forever.

At sunup, the locals found Ivan's boat drifting on the current, but no one ever saw the young man again. Months after his disappearance, Marina married another. This one acquired more catch than the entire village folk combined, and Marina's cupboards were never short of jars stuffed with pickled herring and pots of fish stew. Quickly, she grew famous. People traveled long distances across the countryside to marvel at the dishes rumored to invoke such overwhelming emotion that even the most stoic of characters were known to weep, and there were those among them who claimed that Marina's tears for Ivan made her food taste so extraordinary.

And this is how Ivan's wish was granted, though we shall never know if it made him truly happy.

A Lullaby for Mattie Barker

B. Zelkovich

B. Zelkovich writes Speculative Fiction, anything from dragon hunting and space whales to demon-dealing and ghost tales. She likes to explore human emotions in very inhuman situations. When she isn't escaping through her imagination, she escapes into the wonders of the Pacific Northwest with her spouse and their four-legged son, Simon. Connect with her at bzelkovich.com

WANTED:

Sexton needed for small parish and attached graveyard

Room and Board incl.

Quiet community

$1200/yr

Matilda Barker stood in the center of the village, carrying her suitcase like a shield. She'd never heard of the town, never traveled so far from home, but she had found the ad in the paper and used a healthy chunk of Rosie's gratuity to get there.

The moment she laid eyes on the graveyard she knew it was just what she needed. A task she could pour herself into and forget the listless, grey days since the war ended. The pastor's scrutiny said he had doubts but he offered her the position all the same.

The wet spring gave way to a warm and sunny summer. Mattie had never been much of a gardener, but she spent her days cutting back shrubs and pulling the endless tide of weeds that had claimed the graves for their own.

After a day's hard work, Mattie took her supper in the flat below the belfry and read for an hour or two on the window seat overlooking the sea. Then, once the church fell into the quiet of late evening, she explored the chapel by candlelight. Though she was alone, it felt like sneaking and so it was exhilarating. A secret kept between her and the church.

But the church had more secrets than Mattie realized. Each day she spent tending its needs, each night she shared with it her most guarded, curious self, she drew closer and closer to the truth.

That truth revealed itself in the first weeks of autumn. Mattie sat in one of the oak pews of the chapel, reading a hymnal by candlelight and struggling to remember the tune. She hummed to herself, searching for the notes in the dark.

"You're flat," a voice said.

Mattie dropped the book of hymns and nearly dropped the candle. The flame flickered and wavered and threatened to snuff.

"Careful now," the voice said, so close. "You don't want to burn the place down."

She swung the candle but saw no one. A heavy sigh came from beside her and a gust tore through the chapel, dousing the single flame that lit her corner of the pew.

She blinked at the sudden darkness. She'd never moved through the church without her candle, never seen it in the full weight of the night. Mattie's eyes adjusted to the gentle glow of the moon through the windows and let out a shaky breath.

"See now? Isn't that better?"

Mattie stared at the slight man that sat beside her. He was young, with thick hair that rolled like the sea. He wore a shabby coat with a high collar done all the way up, the buttons shimmering in the moonlight.

Shimmering and see-through.

The pale, translucent man fidgeted with the cuff of one sleeve. "I defended you to the others—don't fall apart at the seams now."

"You're," Mattie swallowed against the shiver in her voice. "You're a—"

"Ghost. Yes. You might have noticed us sooner if you spent less of your evenings in the chapel."

"Us?"

"You think I'm the only one? That'd be boring." He tilted his head back and forth. "Although, it'd be much more peaceful. Do you know how hard it is to keep the tenants in line without a proper sexton?"

Mattie thought she was a proper sexton, or did a decent job imitating one, but perhaps she was mistaken? Though she wasn't sure how one could maintain the grounds so poorly that a ghost had to come chastise you over it.

He cast a critical eye over her. "Come on, then."

"Where?"

"It's time you met the people you work for, don't you think?"

She thought she worked for the pastor, but the ghost seemed certain otherwise. He glided out of the church, rippling through the solid oak door like fish nipping at the surface of a pond. Alone in the frail moonlight, Mattie thought she might have dreamt it all.

Then he poked his head through the center of the door.

"Hop to," he said. "The night's never long enough and they're dying to meet you." He frowned. "Pardon the expression."

Dream or no, Mattie followed after him, the chill damp of the sea air against her skin before she could talk herself out of the madness.

She worried she would lose sight of the spectral man, but he glowed against the rhododendron and roses, brighter for the moonlight. Mattie followed, heedless of the peat moss that matted the hem of her nightgown, or the cold that clung in her chest.

Mattie was proud of the progress she'd made in reclaiming the grounds from the greedy weeds and ferns. Only a handful of graves hadn't been cleared yet, and she'd even begun scrubbing the moss from the engraved letters on some of the older stones.

"You know," said a voice. "Pumice would work better than that silly brush you've been using to scrape away the lichen."

An ethereal man perched on a tall, leaning tombstone, his feet swinging merrily above the ground. He wore a tailcoat and top hat and looked exactly like the Mad Hatter; all dapper and out of place, and pleased as punch at the fact.

"Pumice? Do you want to be erased?" A woman appeared, the opposite of the dapper ghost in every way. Stoop-backed and wiry, she wore a frayed coat and billed cap, with a pipe tucked in the corner of her mouth.

"Some of you don't have names worth remembering," the first ghost said.

"Oh, aye," said the second. "Meanwhile some haven't got a relative left to care."

"You old goat."

"I'll worry what you think when you finally hop off that gauche gravestone and do something about it."

The ghost from the chapel retraced his path back to Mattie. He cleared his throat and the sound sliced through their threats, a fin through water. "This is Matilda Barker, the new sexton."

"Hello, ma'am," said the first. "Reginald Taylor the First, at your service. It's a pleasure to meet you." He smiled at her and flourished his cap in a little bow, tilting forward precariously on the gravestone.

The second glared at Reginald then looked at Mattie. "I'm Regina Taylor the Not-Quite-Second, but you can call me Reggie."

Reginald the First scoffed. "I hate that nickname."

"Why do you think I insist on it?" said Reggie.

The man floated between Mattie and the arguing ghosts. "Come. They'll be at it all night at this rate." Without touching her, he guided her away from the bickering pair and further into the graveyard.

"They're related?" Mattie asked.

"Yes, though," he turned to shout over his shoulder, "Heaven forbid they act like it."

Neither Taylor seemed to notice.

"The Taylors never saw eye-to-eye, in life nor death."

"Hardly seems like a happy story," Mattie said.

He stopped in mid-air, and Mattie might have collided with him if such a thing were possible. "This is a graveyard, Mrs. Barker. And while there are some happy stories, many of them aren't." He spun, gazing at the markers. "The war stories chief among them."

He continued up the path, but Mattie couldn't convince her feet to follow. The words were too heavy. Too true. Her heart raced and her breath came shallow and frantic. She closed her eyes and counted up through ten, then twenty, and past thirty until the shaking in her hands settled.

When Mattie opened her eyes the thin ghost hovered before her, his gaze unsettling in their intensity.

"Do you know what is required to be a proper sexton, Mrs. Barker?"

"A sharp pair of shears?"

He laughed, the sound brittle as seashells. "No. To tend to the dead, one must know death, must carry it in their bones and wear it on their soul like a badge."

They watched one another for a moment, but Mattie couldn't think of anything to say to that. So she nodded, took a deep breath, and bade the ghost continue the tour.

They walked through the graveyard until the pale hint of dawn tinged the sky. Mattie met a ghost for every marker in the graveyard. Every marker except the fresh, gleaming one with flags and flowers at its base.

It was so new, so obviously cherished that Mattie had avoided it out of respect. There were other graves that needed her attention, so she'd spent her days trimming hedges and scrubbing stones.

Now, alone in the murk of twilight sky, Mattie passed the grave and felt a distinct chill. The moisture on the polished tombstone trailed like tears down the front to catch in the sharp lines of the words engraved there.

Here Lies Robert William Boyd
Beloved Son of William and Bonnie
1919–1943

"The war stories," Mattie said, the ghost's words echoing through her head. She'd lived a war story of her own ever since that knock came at their door. A uniformed stranger delivered a letter and a check. As if there were a price tag on life. As if any dollar amount could replace what she'd lost.

She knelt to right a toppled flag against the gravestone, and beyond the pristine granite marker, at the border of the grave-yard where the stones lined the cedars, she saw a flicker of pale light against the shadows.

Then the sun broke through the clouds and snuffed the specters in the light of day.

Since moving into the church, Mattie's days had been long, but her nights had been her own. Now her nights belonged to the ghosts.

Each night a spirit would find her. Perhaps while reading a book, preparing dinner, or to her utter mortification, taking a bath. It mattered not to the residents of the graveyard what she was doing, it mattered only that she listened.

The Taylors joined her for dinner at least once a week, separately of course. And though they couldn't eat, Mattie always set a place for them; it felt rude otherwise. One spirit visited almost nightly to tell Mattie about her concerns for the graveyard, from raccoons to seagulls, all manner of critters worried the anxious ghost.

Fall came and went, her evenings shared with a host of ghosts, each full of stories, concerns, and problems. Mattie became less a groundskeeper and more a caretaker, attending to the residents of the graveyard with more tenderness than she ever had the plants. Always, she strove to make them feel better; whole and cared for. Human.

She did that for all of them. All of them except the ghost of Bobby Boyd.

She lavished his tombstone, polishing it by day and visiting it by night. She wandered the dark grounds, her peacoat pulled tight and her collar high against the early winter chill, but still he never appeared.

Mattie finally decided she would wait him out. She moved the flowers and the flags, now shredded and sagging from the weather, gathered her skirt beneath her and sat with her back against his tombstone. The wind wove through the trees, the coarse branches waving and whispering against one another. She feared she might catch cold if she sat there too long.

"You do know you have to be alive to be a proper sexton, right?" The ghost with the high-collared coat stood beside the grave marker, peering down at her. "You'll do us no good if you die of cold."

"I'm helping."

"A bit late for that."

"He died in the war. I know a little something about that."

He squinted those too big eyes. "You lost someone."

She lifted her chin. "Who didn't?"

They stood in the cold wind and watched one another before the ghost said, "Tell me about him."

"Her," she corrected. "And I'd rather not." She looked away from him. From his inhumanly still face. From the wide eyes that saw everything.

She didn't want him to see the tears in her eyes.

"The war took something from us all," he said once the quiet spread too long between them.

Mattie wiped at her face, but when her vision cleared the ghost was gone.

When the winter winds crashed against the coast, the visits from the graveyard's denizens dwindled. She hadn't expected the weather to affect the ghosts, but even they weren't impervious to the ocean's fury. She'd just grown accustomed to the quiet once more when, while reading a book in bed, she heard the stilted notes of the piano from down in the chapel.

She didn't bother with a candle; after so many nights shared with the specters, she'd grown used to the dark. On bare feet, Mattie moved through the church silent as her tenants. When she reached the chapel a familiar figure in a high-necked coat hovered upon the piano bench, his thin fingers pressing the keys with effort.

It took incredible focus for the ghost's fingers not to go through the keys, so that he could never press more than one at a time. He sat hunched before the instrument, hair heavy on his brow and his mouth set in a line.

Mattie wasn't sure if it was the struggles of the piano that tormented him so, but watching him reminded her just how young the ghost was. Had been.

"I used to play," he said.

She flinched at his voice. His words were sharp, the crack and crumble of boulders turned to rubble. A broken voice for a broken boy.

"When Pastor Evans was out of earshot, which was always since he's half-deaf." He chuckled, a sound dark as the moonless night beyond the windows. "I used to do a lot of things. Swim. Fish. Garden." He turned luminous eyes on Mattie, and though they were large in his thin face, they were hollow and cold. "Care for this graveyard."

Of course. The way the ghosts deferred to him, how he knew so much about the graveyard and its residents. How he'd never told her his name.

"You're Bobby Boyd."

He didn't blink, didn't lick his lips or look away or do any of the million little things the living did without thinking. The ghost of Bobby Boyd hovered at the piano, his hands poised over the keys and stared at her with too bright eyes.

"Not anymore."

He vanished. He didn't dissolve like sea spray caught in the breeze, didn't fade from view like the cape succumbing to the fog. One moment he sat at the piano, a shimmering and sad appa-rition, and the next Mattie stood alone in the chapel, gaping at the ivories and the faint indentations they wore.

She spun the plain gold band around her third finger. She main-tained the grounds, the records, and the graveyard. She was the sexton, and a proper one too. She cared for the ghosts of this graveyard—Bobby Boyd would be no exception.

Days bled into nights, and the winter storms mellowed into the timid cheer of coastal spring. With warmer days came busier nights as tenant after tenant came to call on her after sunset. She convinced both Taylors to join her for dinner at least twice a week, and their bickering gradually turned into conversations. Mattie was certain that, given enough time, they would find common ground. Or at the very least, stop antagonizing one another on a nightly basis.

But of all the ghosts in her care, the one she most desperately wanted to see eluded her.

She thought she saw Bobby Boyd once, late at night, as a glimmer of moonlight against the cedars. She ran across the graveyard to meet him in just her nightgown. But when she reached the trees nothing greeted her but the dark and damp of cedar and salt. And suddenly she was furious. She was here. She wanted to help, and he was just going to wander the woods and mope?

"I know you're out here Bobby Boyd!"

A cormorant warbled at her in irritation, but the dark was otherwise silent.

"And I have to tell you, I'm a little sick of this woe-is-me routine." She glared at the trees, at the moss and the ferns. "I am sorry you died, Bobby. I'm sorry you were shipped off and snuffed out." She winced at the words, her frustration sharpening them more than she liked. "I'd change it if I could." Her voice caught, her throat tight as her eyes stung. "I would undo that whole damn war and you'd all be back where you belong."

The cedars creaked and rustled in the breeze. Even with all the ghosts for company Mattie had never felt so alone. Standing there in the dark, surrounded by the trees and the sea breeze, she had never needed to talk to someone so badly.

So she talked.

"Rosie was a nurse, even before the war. We sobbed when we read about the camps." Mattie would never forget the way Rosie's tears had soaked through the newsprint, smudging the article with her compassion. "She enlisted the next morning."

Alone and crying, she told their story to the night. How Rosie had kissed her for the first time, behind the ice cream parlor. About the private ceremony they'd had in their backyard years later, just the two of them and a friend. How Rosie had never once kept their love a secret, even when the whole town had shunned them for it.

How they'd fought before Rosie left. How Mattie had begged her, pleaded and screamed and demanded. How she threw her words at the woman she loved: "If you love me you'll stay."

How Rosie replied: "If you love me, you know I can't."

She wiped at her cheeks and nose, banishing the tears as more fell. "Then that letter came with the money and I didn't know what to do. Didn't know how to face all the places we'd made memories. I saw the ad in the paper and I—" She shrugged. "I ran away."

"But it didn't work. I still carry Rosie with me. I think about her when I wake up and when I fall asleep. She's never left me—I was haunted before I ever came to this graveyard." Mattie shook her head. "I thought I came to this town to start over, but all I really did was start again. Same heartache, different town."

Mattie wasn't sure what she expected. Maybe that a heartfelt admission of her grief and loneliness would resonate with the ghost. That he'd appear like a mirage out of the trees to tell her she was right. That, thanks to her, he would try to make the best of his afterlife.

None of that happened.

Instead she stood in the dark, shivering and searching the trees for any sign of Bobby Boyd and finding nothing at all. She waited until the tears dried to salt on her cheeks, until her teeth chattered and her hands trembled and she knew she needed to get back inside.

She cast a final glance around the woods and sighed. "You know where to find me when you're ready to talk." She counted to ten, just in case he decided to show his face, and then she hurried back to the warmth of the church.

Weeks went by same as they had before. Dinners with the Taylors and days spent weeding and mulching and scrubbing. The time went quickly enough, the days getting easier as the sharp lance of grief ebbed into the dull ache of memory.

The days were easier, but her worry for Bobby Boyd weighed her down like an anchor.

One night in September when sleep proved impossible, Mattie stood at the window overlooking the coast. She'd opened it before going to bed, hoping the crash of the surf would soothe her anxious mind. But the chill wind prickled her skin and nipped at her fears, whipping her thoughts into whirlpools of doubt. She worried that Bobby's spirit still wandered, that he lingered between the boy he'd been and the ghost he was. She feared that the war would haunt him long after the treaties were signed.

These thoughts consumed her, despite the calm hush of the sea, until a new sound climbed the steeple and floated through her window. A single note, high and chiming. Then another. And another. Until at last they melted together into a simple, lilting melody with the ocean for its guide.

She swayed to the song until she yawned, the notes easing her mind. With the ghost's lullaby floating through the room Mattie returned to bed, a small smile on her face.

Bobby Boyd had come home from the war at last.

Jovis

Kemi Ashing-Giwa & Tali Arima

Kemi Ashing-Giwa is the USA Today bestselling author of The Splinter in the Sky, the forthcoming novella This World Is Not Yours, and several short stories. She studied integrative biology and astrophysics at Harvard, and is now pursuing a PhD in Earth & Planetary Sciences at Stanford. She and Tali have been friends and writing buddies for nearly two decades.

Tali was born and raised in California and currently lives in the Bay Area. Her love of writing began in kindergarten, where she met Kemi and became fast friends and writing partners. Her other interests include animal rights and mental health awareness.

An early version of this story first appeared in Coffin Bell, April 2020.

I should run.

As still as stone, Iyaafin watched the storm roll across the desert toward her. It swallowed up the desert and vomited sand into the burning air.

Run, she commanded herself.

But she was frozen with fascination by what would no doubt be the cause of her death in ten—perhaps fifteen—minutes. The feeling thrumming through her veins was horrible and beautiful; poisoned honey melting over her parched tongue and dissolving in her blood. Was something wrong with her? Or could someone only feel alive as they faced their own end?

The golden behemoth steadily looming over the encampment was somewhere between a wave and a cloud. The closer the storm got, the worse it became. Its belly darkened with wind-fueled rage as it devoured ever greater lengths of the sky, taking on the strangest hue Iyaafin had ever seen. The color of the promise of pain, and like the beast that had birthed it, it scrambled to conquer all that lay before it. It was as if the planet had been torn open and redrawn in its own blood. The storm reared up, blocking out the sun in an attempt to hide its own monstrosity.

A hand clamped down hard on her shoulder, dragging her from her entranced stupor.

"Iyaafin!" The voice was threaded through with steel, and was all but consumed by the tumult. "Turn your back toward the wind, and follow me!"

Iyaafin turned. She faced the captain, the leader of this doomed mission. The captain raised an arm corded with muscle, pointing toward the Ruins. They were barely a reddish smudge through the swirling sands.

"There," roared the captain, the words reduced to a whisper in the wind. "Shelter. We'll be safe there."

***

The captain broke down as soon as they were through the sun-bleached doors, collapsing over the shattered triangular tiles of the chamber. Their strangled gasps ricocheted off the ancient walls of the Ruins' inner sanctum and echoed through crumbling corridors. Iyaafin sat cross-legged at their side, drawing in quiet breaths. The captain had done nearly all the work, forcing themselves through the blistering, brutish winds and carving a path through the storm. Iyaafin had clung desperately to the captain's back, doing little else besides hanging onto her leader's jacket and stumbling after them.

She glanced down at them and wondered, not for the first time, why the captain had volunteered to lead this mission in the first place...especially after finding out she'd been assigned to it, especially after everything that had happened between them. Iyaafin tipped her chin upwards, searching for the ceiling, but the slated ochre walls of their refuge only stretched ever upwards, toward the sky. Toward infinity, it seemed, but shadows obscured the building's progress.

A sudden, visible shudder crawled down the captain's spine, and they curled themselves up into the fetal position. Iyaafin crouched down low, her right ear pressed against the surprisingly cool stone. A sob forced itself from the captain's lips.

"I lost them," they moaned. "I lost them all."

The landing party had been sent down to collect biological samples, take detailed readings, and reexamine the Ruins: the only evidence humanity had thus far uncovered of alien intelligence. The trip into the ancient, half-collapsed structures was supposed to have happened at the very end of the expedition. Technically, they weren't supposed to be anywhere near the Ruins without full envirosuits, but that seemed like the least of their worries.

"You didn't lose them," Iyaafin said, lifting a hand to pat the captain's back. An onyx eye glared up at her from under a dense tangle of black hair. She yanked her fingers back as if she'd been burned. "The storm separated us, but we were the closest to it. If we're alive, then I know they are too." All of this, lies. She knew nothing. "And they know where to regroup."

"The shuttle," the captain said, their voice low and gritty, as if their vocal cords were caked with sand.

"Yes," said Iyaafin. "We'll wait for the storm to pass. Warren said these monsters only last a half a day at most here."

"*Warren*," hissed the captain. "Damn him and damn this planet. If he were half as smart as he thinks he is, we wouldn't be in this fucking mess."

Warren was the mission's meteorologist. He'd taken, it seemed, quite a few liberties on his resume. Iyaafin pursed her lips; perhaps she was being too harsh. No scientist, no matter how clever, could possibly predict the finicky weather patterns of every planet they got stuck on.

"Yes, damn him," Iyaafin agreed, anyway. "But for now, we might as well try to salvage this mission." She paused, considering calling the commander at her side by their name. "...Captain."

The captain flew to their feet, their spine suddenly as straight as the surrounding crimson columns.

"Yes. Lieutenant, what can you tell me about the Ruins? Where should we start?"

Iyaafin felt her stomach sink. She tried to hide her grimace. She was just the astrobiologist, shipped straight from the Interstellar Union's headquarters on Europa. She took environmental samples and then she scanned them for ancient biosignatures. She likely knew even less about the Ruins than the captain. But ever since they'd met at that sticky-floored bar so many years ago— ever since the captain had gotten her talking about the evolutionary wonders of Europan microbes, they had assumed her to be omniscient.

"Well," Iyaafin began anyway. "They were built two thousand years ago. By the very creatively-named Builders. But then the Builders all died, leaving only these here Ruins as proof of their existence."

The captain narrowed their eyes at her, as if attempting to determine if she was jesting. "You know, I've read a book before."

"Sethunya's the archeologist, not me," said Iyaafin, grinning apologetically. "And this is my first time planetside." She waved her hands around, gesturing expansively at the featureless carmine walls. "I've never had to deal with all this...*stuff.* Just small things. Cells and molecules and—"

A sound like crunching ice reverberated through the chamber, cutting her off. They both almost snapped their necks in their haste to look upwards.

"Ever dealt with big things?" the captain guffawed.

Iyaafin turned away in silence.

She peered up into the darkness, and the darkness peered back.

Two shimmering silver-white eyes shone through the shadows, each like a white dwarf burning in the void of space. The captain made a strange gurgling sound, as if they'd wanted to scream and gasp and had tried to manage both.

A strange sensation washed over Alnia, so eerily similar to that which she'd felt when she'd watched the approaching sandstorm. She was caught between all-consuming terror and all-consuming captivation, her blood turning to ice water as endorphins rushed through her. She half-expected her thudding heart to rip itself from her ribcage and start tap-dancing on the tiles at her feet.

Iyaafin had a hand half-raised in greeting when something shot towards her, a blur of white and gray and black. It barreled into her as if she were made of paper and she went flying, the back of her head cracking against stone. It was over by the time she even considered screaming. But her teeth were locked together anyway, the enamel welded by the white-hot spear of panic that lanced through her. Agony blossomed from the bottom of her skull and seared down her spine, setting each and every nerve alight. Her vision splintered and reformed as she scrambled to her feet, flickering black spots dancing across her eyes.

The captain shrieked.

It was the most horrible sound Iyaafin had ever heard. It didn't seem human. It didn't seem like it could have come from *any* animal. It was fear and pain and desperation and sorrow and—and then it stopped, suddenly, with a clean, wet snap.

Iyaafin could see clearly now. She could see the captain's bloodied fingers, curled into claws. And above her leader crouched the thing that had murdered them. It was feasting, the pieces of its hard-shelled mouth giving way to reveal row upon row of needle-thin teeth. Stomach acid lurched up Iyaafin's throat and bubbled over her tongue, spewing from her mouth in a string of violent, strangled coughs. She stared at the thing, her freed teeth sinking into her tongue to keep from screaming. The coppery tang of blood replaced the sting of the acid.

It resembled a flat-bodied isopod, with six segments that darkened from bone-white at the head to an oily black at its tail. Dark red scraps of something that might have once been clothes hung over the creature's curved form. Twelve arms, of various length, cradled the captain, almost protectively. Gently. But it ate as if starving. It probably was. Iyaafin took in its shriveled limbs, its sunken silver eyes.

There were brief, fleeting moments in her life when Iyaafin had wondered if there might truly be some benevolent, omnipotent force in the universe. She knew now that she'd never have another of those moments again. The creature bent low, and neatly plucked the captain's arm from the socket with its teeth.

How could the human body possibly hold that much blood? It was obscene.

She had no doubts about whom the creature would make a meal

out of next once it finished with the captain. Its back was half-facing her. She crouched, feeling around in the swelling darkness for something, anything. Her fingers closed around a chunk of vermillion stone.

Could she fault a desperate creature for surviving? No.

But she would kill this one. Iyaafin sucked in a shuddering breath, leapt across the tiles, and drove the stone between its unblinking eyes, deep into what she could only hope was something important. The thing made a sound somehow worse than the captain's last, that same hiss of crunching ice, now twice as loud and far more grating. It sank into Iyaafin's bones and scraped out the marrow.

Three of the creature's arms latched onto her throat and shoulders and flung her into the stone floor. A wretched scream flew from her throat. Iyaafin kicked and punched wildly, but her strikes did little more than enrage it further. The thing snatched her up, slammed her into the tiles again, and sent her sliding across the floor into another column.

But the pain was nothing now, not under the storm of adrenaline and rage coursing through her blood. Iyaafin was on her feet by the time it reached her. She scanned the chamber for a weapon, for a hiding place, for—

Nothing.

She was going to die.

Perhaps it was the concussion, but she felt a strange detachment from this thought. In fact, her instinct was to laugh, but that didn't seem right.

Her gaze slid to the captain. They were light-years beyond

recognition, their jaw ripped clean off. Gnawed, fractured bones lay scattered about the bloody wreck that was once her leader and long ago her friend. And, before even that, something else. Iyaafin's eyes widened.

When the creature swung three arms at her in a strike that would have broken her back, she dived and flew to the captain's side, the creature scuttling just behind her. Iyaafin lifted a broken bone from the still-warm mess and pivoted on her heel just as the thing lunged at her.

The blade-sharp fragment sank into the soft tissue between the shell of two segments. The creature writhed, screaming, and went silent. Blue blood gushed from the wound and into Alnia's eyes—*burning burning burning*—and she flew back. As she stumbled away, something sharp and slick slid from her side. She looked down. And wished she were dead.

There was a gaping hole where flesh should be, shimmering cobalt fluid seeping from the wound like liquified lapis lazuli. She ran a trembling finger around the edge of the puncture, a whimper escaping her lips although there was no pain—anesthetic, *fascinating*—but the shock and revulsion that roared through her, almost robbing her of consciousness, more than made up for it. There was hardly any blood; it was as if her skin had simply folded in on itself.

Iyaafin tore a length of cloth from the edge of her tunic, wrapped it around her abdomen, and with a low, moaning cry, slid down a column until she hit the floor.

***

North.

The shuttle was north.

Past the end of the endless salt flats, the skeletons of extinct oceans and lakes. Through the hardpan fields, lands of nothing but scorching sunlight and wind that howled over the surface of the rock-hard clay. Around the gaping deflation hollows in the east, where fine sand had been blown away to reveal strange concave outcrops. Across the bone-dry steppes and through the fire-orange rock forms carved by centuries of blown sand.

Chusun, this prison of a planet, had once been a world possessed of biodiversity that rivaled Earth's. But the increasing luminosity of its merciless sun had stripped its surface, peeling back layers and layers of life until there was nothing but sand and stone.

The gravity here was slightly less than that on Earth; the trek north was proportionally less unbearable than it would have been on her home planet. But Iyaafin had been walking for what felt like days now, and she was nearing the end. Of her patience, of her strength, of her will to live—she wasn't certain. Another kilometer and she'd just throw herself into the sand and let her blood seep into it, offer herself up to the starved planet.

Iyaafin glared at the undulating sea of gold before her as she dragged herself onwards. Her tongue felt as if it had petrified in her mouth, and her throat had already forgotten what it felt like to swallow. She had felt hunger before, but starvation was a black hole inside her. Sweat ran down her neck in fat beads, soaking the collar of her tunic as the sun heaped its fury over the broken, beautiful landscape—

You're even more so.

Iyaafin stopped so suddenly she nearly keeled over. She didn't need to turn around to know that the voice had come from within herself, from somewhere deep and sacred and, before, *hers*—

"What?" she whispered, though she already knew.

You're even more so, the voice said again. *Even more beautiful than this desert. And broken, but I'll fix you.*

I've already begun.

She tasted the words almost as much as she heard them. A warm, tingling rush of blood rose to her face, her neck.

"Who—*what* are you?" Iyaafin murmured. But she knew the answer to that question, too.

Her fingers brushed over the makeshift bandages she'd wrapped around her wound.

I'm inside you, said the voice.

"That's where you are, not who," snapped Iyaafin, angry that she wasn't angry and afraid that she wasn't afraid.

It's both, argued the voice.

"You're not...*human,*" Iyaafin said, because she didn't know what else to say. "And you can't even see, can you? You have no concept of what beauty is."

I see you, said the voice. *I see you more than anyone else can, and you're beautiful, Iyaa.*

"My name is Iyaafin," said Iyaafin. "Not Iyaa. Don't call me that."

Well, I like Iyaa. I like it more than Iyaafin. It's prettier. And a pretty creature like you needs a pretty name.

"I—"

Don't argue with me, said the voice, sotto-voce, even as something

246

twisted in her side, sending through her a stab of pain so sharp her vision flashed white. *I'm calling you Iyaa.*

"You hurt me," gasped Iyaa, less actually hurt and more shocked that the thing inside her had hurt her in the first place.

I know, said the voice, mournfully. *And I could hurt you so much more, if I wanted to. Don't make me want to, Iyaa. I'd rather protect you.* A thoughtful pause. *I'm going to protect you.*

Iyaa wondered how exactly the thing inside her could possibly *protect* her, but shoved that thought down as soon as it reared its head. She wondered if it could read her mind. She asked.

Why? What are you thinking? ground out the voice, answering her question. *Are you hiding something from me?*

"No," gasped Iyaa, already bracing herself for another stab of pain. "I wouldn't. I can't. Please, don't—"

You're right, agreed the voice, suddenly sounding very pleased with her. *You can't.* A pause. *I like it when you do that.*

"Do what?" asked Iyaa, whisper-soft.

No answer. She ground the knuckles of her right hand into her wound. Instead of the agony she anticipated, something warm and wondrous radiated from her side, spreading over her like oil in a hot pan. It was as if she were swimming through liquid sunlight. She knew, somehow, that she was being drugged, that the thing was pumping oxytocin and serotonin straight into her nervous system, that this marked the end of her autonomy.

The last vestiges of her self-preservation screamed at her to tear the *parasite* from her flesh with her bare hands, to find the nearest cliff and toss herself over the edge—

But suddenly she was too far gone to care, too far gone now to do anything but *feel*. Her toes curled as another wave of that nightmarishly heavenly feeling fluttered through her, threading her skin with sunbeams.

Beg, said the voice, at last. *I like it when you beg. Now walk.*

And so Iyaa did.

***

She looked at the shuttle. It was less than thirty meters away, a bow-legged beast of steel and aluminum and reinforced glass. Rust-red mountains rose like crimson giants behind it, their scarlet peaks scraping the sky.

"I don't think I should," Iyaa said, finally. "I don't know what'll happen if they know."

Everyone that you know needs to know me too, replied the voice. *I want everyone to know us as we are.*

"I—"

Don't, the voice warned, sending the slightest whisper of pain through her gut.

"All right," Iyaa whispered, though it was anything but.

When she reached the shuttle, she pressed a hand against the identification pad on its side. The sliding doors flew open, revealing a round-faced woman in a pale blue lab coat.

"Evita. Where are the others?" asked Iyaa.

"Nice to see you too," snapped Evita, though she was smiling. "Especially since I was beginning to think you were dead! And not here, obviously." She sighed a long-suffering sigh. "It's just me. I've been waiting for the rest of the team, and honestly—" She cut herself off. "Where's the Cap?"

Iyaa watched Evita watch her.

"Dead."

Evita blinked at her, almost sleepily, and for a moment, Iyaa wasn't certain that the physician had heard her. Mouth pressed into a thin line, Evita slid open a panel in the wall nearest her, revealing a box of rations. She pushed a packet of nutrient-rich crackers toward Iyaa.

"Eat," Evita ordered. "And tell me everything."

Iyaa did. Both were more painful than she'd expected. The doctor's face was a mask through it all, her eyes like stones underwater, reflecting rather than revealing.

"And the thing that killed them...it gave me...it put something—*someone* inside me."

"Medscanner," Evita said, her voice honed to an edge. "Now."

When Iyaa didn't move fast enough, Evita latched onto her wrist, dragged her onto the cot at the back of the shuttle, and shoved her onto her back.

"Lie still," the doctor said, and disappeared behind a protective screen.

"Do you have a name?" whispered Iyaa, once Evita had gone.

I've decided on Jovis. The voice sounded amused. *But you can call me Sun. Only you. I've chosen you, just like you chose me.*

Iyaa's brow furrowed. "I didn't choose you," she murmured.

Maybe not, said Sun. *But you wanted me. You wanted this.*

Iyaa sucked in a sharp breath.

Don't worry. You might not know it yet, Sun continued patiently, *but I do. I know you better than you know yourself.*

The synthetic sheets beneath her were sticky against her skin. Iyaa fidgeted.

"Stay still," Evita hissed through the screen.

"Sorry!" Iyaa called back, sheepish.

What am I to you?

A trap? The question felt like a trap. Iyaa remained silent.

What would I be? If I were human, Sun pressed.

Iyaa swallowed down a hard lump in her throat. "A friend—"

Like the captain used to be, Sun announced. *That's what I want from you.*

Iyaa bit her tongue to keep from laughing.

Ridiculous, she thought, almost fondly.

Evita stepped out from behind the screen then, her datapad hugged against her chest. She was very, very still.

"Do you feel any pain?" she asked.

Iyaa pressed a hand to her side.

"No."

"I need to run a few blood tests," said Evita, pulling a packaged needle from one of the many pockets on her lab coat.

"Fine," said Iyaa, lifting up the remains of her tunic. "Do I need to take off the bandages?"

"Later. I need to know exactly what I'm going to do first," the doctor said, leaning over to admire her friend's handiwork. Her eyes went as round as moons. "Impressive."

Iyaa flushed under the praise. She rolled up the sleeve of her tunic and held out an arm. Evita pulled thirty milliliters of blood in one smooth, sharp motion and slapped on a bandage.

"Did you really need that much?" Iyaa muttered, catching the electrolyte pouch the doctor tossed at her.

Evita's mouth curved into a faint smile as she pulled the needle from the syringe and dropped it onto a tray at Iyaa's side.

"No, of course not." Evita's lips twitched, like she was trying to smile. "I just wanted to cause you maximum suffering."

Iyaa rolled her eyes and watched her friend work, fascinated. Evita divided the blood among four glass plates and slid one under a microscope. At the very back of the shuttle, there was a screen embedded into the wall with a keyboard under it. The doctor stepped over, flicked open a compartment under the screen, and stacked the other plates within it. A low hum filled the shuttle as the computer scanned Iyaa's blood for abnormalities. Evita bent low over the microscope, adjusting the magnification with her right hand and somehow managing to type on the keyboard with the left.

Fifteen minutes later, the computer console spat out its findings. Evita scanned the words, her eyes flicking left and right.

"So," the doctor said, crumpling the results in her hand.

She returned to Iyaa's side and flopped backward onto the cot.

"So," Iyaa echoed.

Evita's brown face had gone grayish, her trademark facade of cheerful bedside manner fracturing apart.

"Well, I have horrible news and strange news and good news."

Iyaa grinned, apropos of nothing.

You seem to like her, Sun noted, the words tinged with something dangerous. *A lot.*

"Tell me in that order," Iyaa said, the smile immediately slipping from her lips.

"The...blade that the creature—"

"I think it was a Builder," Iyaa interrupted.

"And I think you're right." Evita nodded. "I think that the blade was an—"

"Ovipositor, I know. And the egg...hatched, didn't it?"

Evita's eyebrows almost flew off her forehead.

"You can feel...something inside you?"

"Yes," said Iyaa. "Sometimes. What has it done?"

Nothing bad, purred Sun. *I think you'll like it.*

"It's taken your appendix," said Evita, placing a gentle hand over Iyaa's.

"Taken?"

"Eaten."

Oh, Iyaa thought. That was fine. She'd expected something far worse.

"What's odd is that the parasite seems to have functionally replaced it, not that the organ has much use; it even has a little pocket of good microbes for you," Evita continued, her brow only now furrowing with concern—Iyaa schooled her face into something more frightened. "Everything else seems perfectly fine. Actually, if you weren't starving, you'd be healthier than when you left the ship."

See, Iyaa? I'm taking care of you, gloated Sun. *I'm so much better for you than that little bit of meat I ate.*

"The good news is that it's all an easy fix. A small surgical operation," said Evita, "before the parasite takes anything else. It'll be over in less than an hour."

NO.

It wasn't so much of a word as a feeling, screeching through Iyaa and burning her up.

"No," she said, voice low. *"Don't.* I need it."

Evita's gaze softened.

"I know you've been through a lot." Her hand squeezed, reassuring. "But you don't need your appendix to live a perfectly healthy life. And it's gone, anyway. There's only the creature."

Iyaa wrenched her arm away. Evita slid off the cot and faced her.

"Don't touch me," Iyaa snapped. "You said I was better than before!"

"If you hadn't been *starving,* and only for now," said Evita, her voice hardening. "We have no idea what that thing is. I don't have the equipment to run more advanced tests—it could be harming you in ways we don't know yet."

"I need it," ground out Iyaa. "I want it. It's helping me."

"The parasite?" Evita's voice rose, for the first time Iyaa had ever heard. "It's *helping* you? Iyaafin, it's *replacing* you. It's eating you alive, from the inside-out—"

She's lying, she's lying—

"No," Iyaa hissed at her friend. "You're wrong, you're wrong! It wouldn't hurt me, it would never—"

"You said the Builder that attacked you was almost two meters tall!" Evita bellowed. "And you think whatever's inside you is going to remain satisfied with just your appendix? It's—"

"Its name is Sun."

"You named it." Evita's voice had plunged into a whisper. "It's manipulating you, and I'm cutting it out."

Iyaa shuddered. She was too large, too hot. She was going to burst, paint the walls of the shuttle red with her blood.

This is your fault, screeched Sun. *This is all your fault! How could you?*

Evita pulled a new pair of gloves over her fingers and began to prepare an IV of general anesthetic.

"Don't take it!" Iyaa pleaded, almost forgetting to breathe. "Let me have it!"

When Evita turned back to look at her friend, her eyes were wide with—pity? Remorse? Iyaa couldn't tell, and didn't care.

Kill her.

The thought was so strong and so loud that, at first, Iyaa wasn't sure if she'd come up with it herself.

"No," she whispered, even as she slipped off the cot and took one halting step toward Evita, who almost immediately shifted backwards.

It's me or her, said Sun. *You can't have both. You can never have both.* There was something wild in his voice. Something almost human. *I don't share.*

"I can't," cried Iyaa.

"Can't what?" whispered Evita, her back hitting the wall of the shuttle. "What's wrong?"

I love you, cried Sun, even louder. *I took the organ you needed least on purpose, because I care about you. After everything I've done, why can't you be grateful? Why can't—*

"I just can't," Iyaa moaned.

"Iyaafin?" Evita's brows knitted in confusion and concern. "What's going on?"

Kill her! Sun screamed. *She wants to separate us. She's going to murder me! Why can't you do this one thing for me? For us?*

Evita reached out, her fingers curling into a firm but gentle grip around Iyaa's wrist.

"Tell me—"

"I'm sorry, I'm so sorry." Distantly, Iyaa felt tears well in her eyes and spill over. "I have to kill you. I have to, I—" She cut herself off. It was as if she'd been torn from her body, as if she were merely a specter observing herself. "Well, it doesn't matter now."

Evita froze. Her eyes were too round, her eyelids pulled back too far. Her lips trembled, trying and failing to form words.

An observer in her own skin, Iyaa reached back and felt her fingers curl around something sharp—the needle.

***

I'm so proud of you, murmured Sun, after. *You did so well today.*

"Thank you," said Iyaa.

I love you, Sun said. And then, after a moment, *Now say it back.*

"I love you too," said Iyaa, wiping blood from her hands over the front of her tunic.

She pulled up the hem and tore off the bandages. That glittering cobalt liquid had crystallized around the wound, preserving it. Protecting it. It was beautiful.

She was beautiful.

Get up, said Sun. *Get back in the shuttle. Find something heavy and sharp.*

"Why?" Iyaa breathed out.

There were more of you, said Sun. *I want to meet them.*

So this, thought Iyaa, *is how it ends.*

***

Jovis wanted them to be safe. It wanted to protect her. It cared.

If it didn't, it would have just killed her. It would have used her and let her die. But it hadn't, it had sacrificed himself to become part of her. To sustain her. And this was the least—the absolute *least*—she could do for it in return.

But she couldn't. Not now, at least, not while she was heaving up what felt like half her blood volume.

You're overreacting, Sun scolded her. *This really isn't nearly as bad as you think it is.*

It was probably right.

Her body screamed in protest as she struggled and failed to stand. She collapsed. She couldn't move.

You need to get up, said Sun. *You need to find them. Before they find you, or they'll tear us apart. They'll kill me. They'll kill you, for what you did to that doctor.*

Iyaa closed her eyes.

Hadn't it told her to kill Evita?

Hadn't it *made* her?

But she couldn't remember. Blood spilled over her lips and sank into the sand between her fisted hands.

I know you're sick, but I'll make you better, Sun told her. *I promise I'll make you better. I will.*

"How?" Iyaa cried.

Sun was silent, as if taken aback.

It's like you don't trust me, it hissed, shocked.

Far away now, the mountains blurred into small, angry brush-strokes, bleeding across the pale canvas of sky.

"I think Evita was right," Iyaa choked out, each word punctuated with a strangled gasp. "I think you're killing me."

How could you even say that? It sounded hollow, as if the air had been sucked from its lungs. Which was impossible, because it was inside her, where it could not breathe. *How could you even think that?* Its voice rose. It was screaming now. *You're making me upset.* It made a sound like crunching ice. *So after I fix you, after this is all over, you're going to give me something that'll make me feel better again.* It sounded so sweet, now. *Maybe a kidney.*

"What?" Iyaa forced out. "Sun—"

You have two, my little hypochondriac. You only need one.

"I'm sorry, Sun. *Please.*"

"No." Its voice was harder than lonsdaleite.

"I trust you," Iyaa cried. Tears ran down her face, burning. "I do. I trust you more than anyone. More than myself. I—I'm just so scared and so lost and I'm so, so sorry. Just, please don't—"

Fine. She could hear the smile. *Because I love you so much.*

Iyaa swallowed a whimper.

Manners, Sun scolded, its tone toeing the edge of playfulness. *I'm letting you be selfish.*

"Thank you," said Iyaa.

She could feel the answering tide of its satisfaction; its pleasure bubbled up, crested, and flowed over and into her. Its joy was her joy. It was hers and she was its and she could no longer discern where it ended and she began.

Good girl, Sun said. *On your feet. We're going hunting.*

***

She found them on a stretch of desert pavement, the mosaic of interlocking pebbles glittering with shards of rock varnish. She watched them from her perch upon an outgroup, observed their shadows stretch as the sun sank below the horizon. They huddled around a pathetic fire.

Weak.

Iyaa felt a broken smile crawl over her face. The cold was nothing to her now. Everything was nothing, except for Sun.

She narrowed her eyes, refocusing. There were three of them: Sethunya the archeologist, Lan the engineer, Warren the meteorologist. They'd made such slow progress because Warren had broken his leg during the sandstorm, forcing the others to take turns carrying him.

Kill him last, ordered Sun.

Iyaa nodded; Lan was the greatest threat by far. He was stronger than Sethunya and Warren combined. But like his companions, Lan hadn't had sustenance in perhaps a week. Iyaa ran her tongue over her teeth. This would not be difficult. She crept over the packed stone of the desert pavement, shiv in hand.

Be careful, Sun whispered sweetly. *If you die, so do I.*

"I know," Iyaa murmured back, her smile soft.

Then she leapt.

It all happened so quickly.

Lan turned at the last second, so the blade sank into his shoulder instead of her neck. He screamed, blood gushing down his tunic. Lan swung an arm at Iyaa, catching her on the side of her jaw. Iyaa ducked below the next blow and struck out, her blade sinking between Lan's ribs. Iyaa stumbled backwards, fingers tightening around the shiv as Lan crumpled to the sand, gurgled, and lay still.

"Iyaafin," gasped Sethunya, eyes wide with horrified recognition.

Her gaze latched onto her. She'd all but forgotten about the archeologist. She hadn't even moved. She sat eerily still, as if she'd been temporarily turned to stone and her flesh was only just beginning to return. Iyaa lunged toward her, blade held high.

"No!" screeched Warren, from where he lay, useless. "Don't do this! Iyaafin!"

Sethunya scrambled backwards, tripped, and landed on her back. Laughing, Iyaa pounced on her.

"No! Stop! Please, Iyaafin!" she screeched, working in vain to throw her off.

Iyaa's lips curled, baring her teeth. She drove the shiv into Sethunya's foot, and then her thigh, and then her stomach as she crawled upwards. The woman's terrified screams became strangled cries. She was making this hard.

Iyaa's lips curled into a sneer. "*Shut up—*"

She felt rough hands curve around her throat. Her feet lifted off the ground, and she thrashed wildly, but to no avail.

Lan.

You should have slit his throat, screamed Sun.

But she hadn't, and now she was choking, gasping for air that would not come. She clawed at Lan's fingers, and had nearly broken free when something blunt and heavy struck the back of her head. Her last thoughts, as the darkness pulled her under, were not her own. They were Sun's:

Say you love me again, it screamed. *Say it! Say it. Say it. Say it*—

***

Iyaafin came to with a strangled cry.

Her eyes darted around the strange chamber, taking in the too-bright glow of the yellow lights overhead, the pale blue of the walls, the seamless cobalt floor. Familiarity flooded through her then, riding an undercurrent of agony sanded down by anesthetic. She was in sickbay, back aboard the starship *Timoclea*, safe and sound and bound to a bed. And she was missing something.

A man cleared his throat. Iyaafin would have turned to pinpoint the source of the sound if her head hadn't been strapped to the mattress. She looked as far as she could to the left, straining her neck.

There was a doctor, standing a meter or so away. He peered at her with half-lidded eyes, his mouth twisted as if struggling to contain a yawn. He held a datapad.

"You're finally awake," he said. "You've caused quite a bit of trouble, my dear."

"Where is it?" Iyaafin forced the words from between gritten teeth. Everything *ached*—her toes, her back, her neck. Her head, most of all. "Where's the parasite you cut out of me?"

"Don't worry about that," said the doctor. "We took care of it."

"Tell me," roared Iyaafin.

A single eyebrow lifted on the doctor's face, though he seemed unsurprised.

"The lifeform is back where it belongs," he said, his gaze flicking down to his datapad and then back up to her. "On its homeworld."

Iyaafin forced in a breath.

"You let it go free?" she whispered, though she wanted to cry and scream and—

"It was the last of its species," the doctor said slowly, as if explaining a simple matter to a simple child. "We couldn't just kill it."

No, a voice inside her—*hers*—screamed.

She was ablaze, shock and rage flowing through her like magma. Her fingers curled into fists, nails cutting bloody crescents into her palms.

"Lan and Sethunya," Iyaafin said, finally. "Warren. What happened to them?"

The doctor neared the bed.

"They saved you, even after your...savagery. They dragged you back to the shuttle, flew you back here." He smiled down at her, teeth gleaming. "My team was required by law to treat you."

Iyaafin's eyes drifted shut. They should've left her. Or better, killed her, so at least she could have taken that...*thing* down with her.

"They're fine," the doctor continued, drawing ever closer. "You, on the other hand, will spend the rest of your life where you belong, rotting away in some lunar prison for what you did to Evita. We know *everything*. You wouldn't stop talking, no matter how much anesthetic we administered."

"Then you know it wasn't my fault," whispered Iyaafin. "It, *Jovis*—"

"It *was* your fault," snapped the doctor. "You invaded its natural habitat. If you don't wear a full envirosuit you're basically asking for it—"

"That did *not*," Iyaafin hissed, "give it the right to do what it did to me. To my friends."

"The right?" The doctor's smile stretched. "It's just an animal, Iyaa, it'll do whatever nature requires of it. Aren't you supposed to be a scientist?" His tone was equal parts saccharine and scornful. "This never would have happened if you had been more—"

"Careful?" offered Iyaafin, the word less than a whisper.

"Yes," said the doctor, turning away. "That."

He left her there, in a darkness blacker than the space between stars and a silence so deafening she almost drowned.

And as Iyaafin shattered, she thought: *I should have run.*

THANK YOU TO OUR SUPPORTERS

Many thanks to our patrons and supporters, especially:

Johanna Levene • Kate Boyes • Wichael Tellez
carol shoemake • Cathrin Hagey
Natalie Weizenbaum

S Klotz • Amy Meng • Alex grehy • Alina Kanaski
Myz Lilith • Erik DeBill • Frederick Stark
Bonnie Warford • Salomao Becker • Anna O'Brien
Martin Cohen • J'nae Spano • Tory Hoke

Matthew Bennardo • EM Gaucher • Thomas Moulia
Elana Gomel • Maria Brekke • Ana Wang • Lorna D Keach
smokestack • Lisa Short • Sian Jones • Kristina Saccone
BethOfAus • J. Askew • Dirck de Lint • Wanda • Karen
Anderson • Charlotte Nash-Stewart • Liz • Suzanne Thackston
Jen G • Emily Anderson • Maria Haskins • GriffinFire

Want to see your name here? Become a patron!
patreon.com/lunastation

About the Cover Artist

Harkalé Linaï is a French artist and freelance illustrator who creates painterly, colourful illustrations, playing with brushstrokes and organic shapes to build dreamlike pictures.

Her work is inspired by the beauty and wonderful diversity of our world and by the amazing art created by countless artists—from anonymous cave painters to impressionists, from modern-day comic artists to carvers from millennia ago...and also by far too many evenings spent reading fantastical literature or playing role-playing games

harkale.art

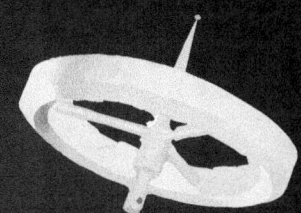

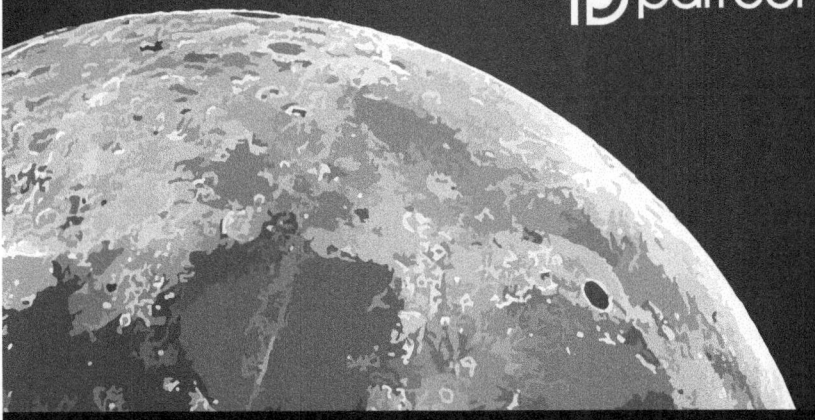

www.ingramcontent.com/pod-product-compliance
Lightning Source LLC
Chambersburg PA
CBHW070813180626
46818CB00001B/251